PHILOSOPHY OF THE SKY

EVAN ISOLINE

CONTENTS:

And since then I've been bathing in the Poem
Of the Sea, star-infused and churned into milk
Devouring the azure greens; where, flotsam pale,
A dreaming drowned man sometimes descends.

Arthur Rimbaud, *The Drunken Boat*

I'm a person. I'm a man. I am neither. I'm over us. I am over myself.

PART ONE

✳

CUBICULUM/SHARK ATTACK

The first thing was the color blue.

The sun's face, I hear the waves rolling across, and at the same time I see a large shark jaw grow on the top of the sun in a geometry of white fire.

The object is itself.

I make the face of the female; her smile is a grim mask. I get lost in my painting of water in a dark room. The camera is rolling.

It's only me and the image that I control, the one whose words cause the sharks to swim around. When I look at the room it's not so much a visualization of the room as it is a visualization of my own fantasies. This is my room in the sea.

I walk into the room. The camera is slowly walking forward, and I can almost imagine that it's going to fly up and into the sky. The room is suffused with dark underwater light. There is a single square window that opens onto the desert. I open my mouth as if to say something. I don't know why there aren't any words. I was so close.

And the erotic image of myself will be the image of the mouth of a shark.
This is a sort of hallucinated sex between me and the ocean.

This isn't the way these words have sounded before. The air is hot with the scent of a rotting fish.

I drew the shark jaw on the wall in black grease.
There is a beautiful young woman in an evening gown dancing at the center of the room.
On the walls I project videos of shark attacks.
The desert is alive with these images.

The sky is a mask.
The object, a decoy.

The woman dancing at the center of the room and a desert filled with white noise. The desert is also completely filled with black smoke. The ocean comes from my mouth and the white noise of the desert. I'll take my own words and the ocean and get lost in the sound
and drown myself beneath the shark's roar.

The white noise of the surf lapping at my ears. The water turns red.

I draw the shark jaw which is my own mouth on the wall as I feel the breath on my neck.
I take my clothes off as I gaze at the mouth of the shark.
The young and beautiful woman takes off her dress in front of the images.
I take my clothes off as I stare at the images with the nude woman blurring in the foreground
of the aquarium-like room.

The conditions of the room dictate my thoughts and my actions.

The ocean is alive now with its own new sex.

I do a few sketches to understand what a shark mouth looks like, finger painting
with black grease on the blue projections of water.
I look at the woman while I write the text on the wall, and I see a scene
[the shark jaw] I write the words "In the water" in a circle.

It is the ocean that is swimming in my mouth
the images will be there to satisfy my mind and my soul until there is nothing left.

The shark jaw reminds me that this is what it means when I look at the sky.

I see in *blue* a prayer beyond the solution to our human problem.

A prayer to the body.

The female is looking at the camera with a bored expression. I get lost in my painting of water in a dark room. When I see her moving to another place, in her eyes, into a deeper aspect of herself, which is the sky, the camera pans to the corner of the room. I begin to associate the image I make of her body with the moving images of the shark attacks.

The sound is very subtle but seems to emanate from a small radio placed on a nearby table in the corner of the room. Next to the radio is a photograph of a woman in a straightjacket.

I put my hand in front of the projector-light filling the room with its shadow. I make my hand into a shark.

The ocean is a black box containing nothing.

I'm looking into her eyes like a deer in the headlights. She's looking at me from underneath an eyelid, almost like a mask.
I have a good laugh.
I feel the warm hand on my shoulder.
I make the face of a man who has just been born.
I make the face of the male.
I make two faces at once, as if I were an observer.
She goes to the window and stares toward the horizon.

I do it again. Another set of lines and lines and lines.
This thick black grease. I make the finger-painting of the shark jaw and the woman and me.
And the room.

The sun has no teeth.

The desert has no language that I know of.

Two more sets of lines.

I have my mask on now.

The sex of the original object (the woman), is now replaced by the image of the shark's mouth.
The source of arousal (the young woman in the room dancing and becoming naked) is contra-
vened by the image of the shark's mouth. I imagine the woman's body is the sky at the moment
that the sky goes from blue to red and back again. This allows me to create a powerful symbol of
climax. At the same time, the shark jaw also signifies the orgasm. The shark jaw is also a symbol
of ejaculation. I make this drawing of the sky as the face of the woman with the shark jaw so that
I can use it as a symbolic masturbatory locus. I splice the two images (the nude woman with the
shark jaw) in my mind by imagining a room. The room is doubled as the sky and tripled as the
sea. The desert is my castration.

Connecting the images. The smell of the grease and the texture between my fingers is making me
sick.

The woman opens the window. I pause in a cinematic gesture of horror. A holographic blue shark
comes in through the window, it's still alive but moving slowly and glitching and it appears like
someone has hot-glued plastic bags into its mouth.

The sun is in the middle of the room.

Here are the thoughts of the desert that I have left behind
white noise is being played on my phone, for the aid of relaxation.

The woman is a woman from my memory.

The woman can swim but I can't.

In my painting we are both wearing masks.

The desert waves are like a loud waterfall in the room of my mind.

Multiple sharks are moving together in a single wave and she is frozen in the image of them all.
But it's just a mask. The image of the sky is the mirror of her and all who enter the tide are frozen
in the image of the sky. I cannot know the thing that I am frightened by. Because it cannot exist
outside of the emotion (room) that gives it a mask. This is what the ocean is like and this is what
you are feeling now. I'm at the edge of the world and the world is what I am.

I press play on myself.

I open my mouth as if to say something. I don't know why there aren't any words. I was so close.

Blue is objective and thus self-destroying.

I remember a window / the psychosemantics of seawater.

Maybe I remember / the theater was a blue cube and transformed into squares / a 4D hypercube
/ [the melody of becoming an individual's subjective trauma] the conceptualization of self that /
is projected onto an object /in a room of white noise.

I think subjectively and the water turns red.

The sky has all the elements for the sexual act. The sky is filled with all kinds of things, the shark
is the subconscious of the object of desire. Therefor I call the sky a "theory."

I whisper, "desert." The sand is cold and smooth; it's as if it's frozen solid, and it feels like death.

I draw the desert as a rectangle.

The shark jaw makes the arousal in the eye the most unspeakable object present in the room full of white noise – the idea of the woman as a decoy — shadow puppet of the shark mouth and stars of grease

I paint stars on the walls.

I turn the image around. In my mind I gaze through a mask of objectivity.
I put my hands on the shark jaws.

I'm trying to figure out how to link this woman and the image of the shark with the image of the sky. The sky is the symbol of the universe. The sky is an image that links me to everything else. When I start connecting things all over the place, I don't believe in the world. 'The World" ends.

Blue is a system/ a landscape /
objectified/ like / a forest
on fire.

The image of the sky inside the image of the woman, and the shark's jaw connected by the words "the sky." So, the shark and the sky each have an identity present in the image of the woman in the desert of my imagination. The sea and the sky can both be objects of worship and of hate.

The shark is a metaphor for the unconscious. This is not to say that I am creating an image of myself to represent the shark. We are both represented and imaged by the woman.

I draw a horizontal line of grease from the middle of the shark jaw around the room, pixels of digital blood projected into my eyes, around the room to where the woman is standing, to the base of her head, and draw upwards, across the ceiling and back down to the window.

I enter the water alone.
I will be a fish swimming through the water.
The ocean is my desert.

A self-inflicted, objectifying, unalterable, subject-causing, uncontrollable/causal object of desire.

I step to the edge of a cliff and jump. I jump into the water. I step to the edge. I dive into the blue sky. Then I swim through the water.

I have painted the mouth of the shark of this constellation because it is the shark of my body and the shark of my mouth that will destroy the image of myself. The woman in the room is not a woman. The woman is the object representing the sky that I sacrifice myself to.

Because /I/ am like that

I will always lose

I will never get my wish

I will never be eaten by a shark

because I will eat myself

I will eat myself because I will starve

I will starve for the love of the thing that will kill me.

Blue is a fractal.

I find the image of myself painting the naked woman black with grease as symbolic of the death of the subject. The image of subjecthood is a symbol of the resurrection of the object, or the creation of something new from something already known.

I know it was an act.

Desert

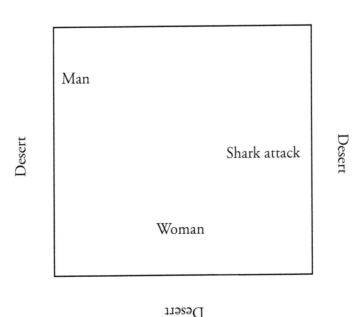

Desert

Man

Shark attack

Desert

Woman

Desert

Desert

The desert noise is making it more real for me, as if the desert represents the end of the world. The sky is bright, I think of it as the sky, but I could see the sun through the smoke of a desert. I smear the wall with a picture of a fish, I can't be afraid, because the fish will help me see it coming.

It's only as I paint the word "BLOOD" that the photograph on the table changes into a photograph of a naked man with a mask on his head. Because of this, the image of the dancing woman's face is replaced by the face of a shark. I get lost in my painting of water.

I paint the sun in black grease.

I like the image of the shark attack because for me it simulates the ultimate erotic act. In approximating death, the scenario presupposes at least two sets of conditions of objects that are opposite each other, moving toward the crowning, inevitable violence of non-duality. I can't tell if it's raining or how beautiful the sunset might be, but I'm looking at the sky, because I was thinking about the fact that I only have six senses, and I feel like I could add a few more. But the shark attack is just a mask, and this is what excites me.

The clouds are being eaten.

I begin to associate my drawing with a much more active form of voyeurism.

Shark attack-suicide as sex act is not a fantasy you seek,
rather it is the truth from which you will be made ill.
I look upon the woman
she is moving towards me
the woman moving through the room,

(the interior of a cube / or the

real identities of / the / sky)

is a living embodiment of the shark.

And there is that thing that I can hear—a sound.

This painting has the look of an empty room where the walls are made up of psychic images and you're trapped in a sort of loop of the mind. I like the sound "shark jaw" and the arousal of fear I get from the videos. The painting I have made is a masterpiece and is so beautiful I begin to cry.

I look at the sky. In the image of the sky I conjure the image of the woman turning into a man. I put my hand in my mouth and bite down, because I am a shark.

I will show you how I love you.
The door of the dream will open.

The painting of the water is so beautiful and you are so full of water in your sleep and everything is wet, the shark jaw as the face of the sky, hallucinations in the desert, [the ocean sounds], I create a picture that will hunt me, that will smell my blood.

I paint over the window. I can't stop now. I paint it out. I scoop up handfuls of grease. I paint out my face. I paint out the whole room. I can't stop now.

And suddenly, in that moment, I pause the room.

BLACK.

The sky flashes down.

Narrow window frame.

I change masks.

I don't know why there aren't any words.

The window / and the 'object' within /

I swim through / the shark jaw of eternity

I think of her / she lies soft under my mask

/ I'd become the sun and drown my mouth in gore

I would be the object reflected

A crystallography—
an ode to the void
—or a call to an unmade peace—
—but of a different kind / an acolyte's call.

The object that contradicts itself / the object is a paradox and thus/is/at/the/same/time/ in that state of complete self-death.

These are real images
these are my own creations for use in a sexual fantasy
my eyes are closed and this is how I came.

This is how I chose to experience all of this.
If I look at shark attacks now I will do it.

I will see the shark jaw.
I will see its nakedness
at the moment of death.
Against the blue.

The second thing is everything else.
I wonder where you go from here.

I am going to make something that makes me.

I'm going to create a monster.

PART TWO

✳

EARTHLESS
(monster of mine)

I re-membered him
a body I had once seen
a room I'd been in

I found him
an object that I needed

And how the thing that kept my eyes fixed shall return
and how I am the god of that thing, its place of origin.

When I look at my new body, my other body
I stand in front of him, scream
I scream to fill the void of silence in his body

The blossoms of blood against the screens
the dew spews
the sounds of the moth

I catch the sky
on the eye of death's face

And the monster in me feels the same

I scream at the bridge of space between us
My scream is a demonstration

I watch him there
mouthing a dead word that has no meaning
as if inside a dream

I try to make out the word

(A song he learned from the most dangerous animal,
a new word for God?)

I repeat the anamorphic syllable, as he looks at me dumbfounded

"not"

I am the new word outside itself
a word for a god that has replaced me

He gives a sound to me
He gives me a name

Now I am just a word, created in the negation of my being
'Wow' I think
Now I must destroy him

I am Not
I cannot be, but I must be
mouthing a word that has no meaning, he says
that I am this person, this being, this "God"
that I am *not* a person
outhing a word that is the negative of 'to be'
He says
I am not myself

It's true
that I didn't want to be "me" anymore
So, I divided myself—I split myself in two
But the longer I am around him, the more I want to kill him
because he becomes more and more like me

He is like a shadow   a reflection   a double of me

I call him my friend, my son
but he has quickly become my enemy
because I hate myself, for what I have become

I am him and he is me
and two is too many

I repeat it again
and then again
as it doesn't seem coherent
He looks at me, eyes tethered, drawling out the word
My first attempt I tried to give it a meaning
the word had a few different sounds
like "not" or "that"
but every time I try to give the word a meaning
it is the same
like "I am not" or "I am that"

I either don't exist or I am an object
Insentient
A cell stuck in telophase

I am a monster inside my second self
and I can no longer see, having licked the candle to death
inside this meat-dark labyrinth
with some thing that resembles me

From a single word, I'll become what the person who makes me is not

They say that you are what you create
I am the monster's first word
I'm the dream of an inanimate object
sent to myself as a warning

I thought the monster would make me happy
but now I realize
I want to be who made *me*
to meet who I'm a monster of

I want to have made myself
I hate myself for this

I wish I knew you before you made me
Wanting to disappear, behind the curtain for good
I look at this monster I've made
this replicant born of annihilating boredom

I know I am going to die for it
I made the monster so I didn't have to unmake *myself*

But he will kill me, and I will kill him
I'm in a nightmare
pressed inside the mirror

The monster standing before me
not me, but an approximation of my body
the simulation of a living thing
'I'm so real—I'm more than real'

I want to let it die so I can take a break
from myself
I think about it, but I'm scared to do it
I'm afraid of the thoughts he inspires in me

I think of a kind of sex that I couldn't have
a suicidal form of masturbation
I'm sick of being with myself, the monster of me

I have reproduced nothing but my own discontinuity
(the reason why I want to be killed is because I do not want to be killed)
If I kill him, I kill myself

I have hermaphroditically negated myself with a word
I made a word into a gesture
I do not want to see God face-to-face
and yet I will be the slave of God
This is the mitosis of having fucked yourself to death

My name is Not

I can't help thinking of fucking myself
I am here
I'm the only thing in this world that can make himself feel better

I think about my father
I see him all dressed up

I look at myself in the mirror
I can see my mother in that mirror

I know it was a mistake

I want to live forever and think about all the times I couldn't
I want all of my family to know I lived forever
even if my resurrections were accidental

I think of how I'm still not sure if I'm living or dead
I want my name to be known
broken but not all the way

Prepare to meet God
I induces Thou

My mind is a hollow shell, I find imaginary hues inside
the pain of becoming myself is intolerable
Pain is the color blue

I think about my father
I think of how I wanted to tell him
that we all die by our own hand

I think about the blue, I scream until the sky goes out
and I'm just screaming over the radio static
over the noise of a color

I think of my mother
her green duress
and how I never returned what I took from her
my fugitivity straight from the womb

I miss her
whose eyes looked back through the holes of a balaclava
lit by the fires of our burning city

Green
I think of how violent
the color green really is

Like the song of the whale, the shell is about to speak
Like if orgasm was a sound and not a feeling
the primitive blue opening of a mouth
the crackling shell of my mind
with tiny little teeth like those of a monkey
flopping open

I get very close to my monster
I map the vulnerabilities on his nude flesh
I wanted to make something that would make me
but now I can see that his fate was to replace me
because he will seek meaning in his existence
He will defy the boundary of my blueprint of him

Now I see that fate is real
Fate is only the paradox of finding yourself
where you were told you would never be

Slowly, he points to himself
He wants to know his own name
Who he *is*, who *he* is.
I ask him what he would like to be called
He looks off, out the window with fear in his eyes
He looks back

His eyes now turgid with desire
like two empty rooms filling with a beautiful music
or floodwater

He begins to mouth a word
He moans and drools clumsily over it
The word finishes as if followed by a thousand periods
He says, "Maaaachhhhhiiiiiiiiiiiiiinnnnnnne"

He is Machine
The system created by nothing
I did not understand the consequences of my actions
until this moment, so, I must destroy my creation
Fear created the monster in the first place, not me
and now *I* am the monster born of this fear

I created you to give myself purpose, but I have only manifested my fear
of having my purpose taken away
and now I'm taking it back. I 'm leaving you out in the wilderness
of my self

I'm not sure if the monster will survive the wild
I'm so angry with you in the same way that I am angry with myself
for not being certain of who or what you are
for being an offspring of fear itself

The world we live in is a war between two
the first self and the next one
It's a war between something fixed and something moving

The mind whispers:
There is a word for everything
There is a word for every thing

The world I live in is a war between selves
and yet it seems that, in the mirror
I am still in the basal state
where every object has a personification

A thing I am, a creature
an act I do
an eye I see
an object I become
I see myself in everything, *in every thing*

An inanimate object whose double has been replaced by
a single word
creating a triple, a triangle
a single line fractured in two places

You are the child of the couple who saw the war begin
Your enemy is the word
The word that started the war

I'll try and kill myself once I've invented a new language for sex, a new word for 'you'
What if I was nothing more than a dream inside your body

I'm afraid of t(he)e
I'm who you were
Not who you are

Maybe fathers just can't create quite as well as mothers
Maybe the sky had fallen a long time ago

The dream is a line that will never touch itself
The wet dream of a word that can't find its body

I remember when I was a monster
They showed me how to write
I wrote like I was taught
I'd seen them write with their fists on piano keys

I drew circles and numbers on the wall, and they asked me to write my name
I didn't know my name—I wasn't given one
I drew a large X

The X was me
They carved an X on my face
and they said, "I give you battle" and my tongue moved along

I look at my creation now
I ask him where he comes from
He says that the devil brought him here

To this I wept, scientifically
on the floor of this dark and quiet church
But the music was so sweet, the music of his indelicate words
that I began to sing, silent as a shoreline

They used my eyes to carve images
of myself

To create me (make me) out of flesh

They couldn't seal off the holes they put in my head
They made a wax mold of my mouth
but I spit it out

What are you doing in this room and not in other rooms?

The dark frost clangs

I know you love me more
when I say: "I Love You"
I know how selfish life is

and I know that the universe is just a bunch of things mashed together
I want to become the center

Beneath the girders of plastic snow
I'm in this endless future, I see the flowers detonated
I see the flowers

parabolic

to go up and away, or to come down and back, in relation to some fixed object or place

parallax

parallelism that occurs when two points cross at the same angle; an entrance that is also an exit

apostate

the plane of a disk that has a fixed orientation relative to a horizontal plane; vertical dismemberment

elegy

hermaphroditisms are not separate things, but the other half of the same thing

I must live

I believe myself

I have been to Paradise

The devil is dead

God told me

But my God isn't real   I think he's my mother I have all his pictures on my phone

I have no life I don't wanna be here

The sun is going down I'm tired I hate this

I love you   I am your father (my son)

All this is meaningless

I'm in a hell You'll see it for yourself

I'll stop when I can feel no pain   You're wrong   It hurts now   Why did you do that

I guess you're wrong   My son   Me

My God is dead   And all these years and everything that you made

All while erasing the ground beneath your feet

I'm here

I'm here and I'm sorry

I'm here because you told me to be

You think I'm crazy   I'm too good for that   I'm so sorry

In the town square, the new Machiavellian
Voice of the future
Voice of the occult

The re-Earther
The lunatic god sent to blow up the cubic plane
The lunatic god in insect hell
Eating through the ceiling

I'm inside the invention of the self
The template of a priority
begging the world to let me be

dehumanized

A casualty and absorbency of the continent
An identity ripping out of its host-body

Midnight ten years later
One thousand years later

No difference

Non-influence in the variables of time
and a finitarian species of love

maybe motherly

I look at my monster

I look at me

I see the twinned signs of madness, and know, from the expression in his eyes

that men will rise against him

their faces blue as they dance to the rhythm of murder

I put a ski mask over his head

The face: it's gone

a familiar face is a bad sign

we should start fresh

I feel like a mother

I didn't ask for much
A tongue, a souvenir
a meteorite lodged in my head

They moved the X away from the hole
and they started to laugh as the first word came out
each word beginning with the letter X

A ball of gauze
for the smoldering hole that it left
(something they called "the mouth")

There it is

The dinosaur breath
something that is infinite's time running out

a spider
websick

a crowd watching

A quintessence of hate for the word 'motherfuckin'
Nope-pulse in a hollow hole
The tang of dirt

I scream
I scream and if we have no sky, all the images beneath it will vanish at once

I think of my childhood
fogging back into night
The whole, the hole, the monster and me
the pale green
nibbler of the sky (two-sided)
Honey-splashed
boy
and the smell, the vomit

But the future is not an area of action that brings pleasure
the future is written like history
the haunted cubicle is not its center

I love this feeling of being inside myself
my ears are popping

.

The swept wind and the green sky blinking
The sky does not know how to leave my mind
the clouds in the sun-heated sea

What is here is not real
hunted, lost or dying
Just look past the faces urgently X'd out
They are not 'you' they said
Now I tremble for the birds to play
His first word was a word that had no form
His mouth looked like the glassy-pink gash of a shell
I'm not talking about the sleepiness
But still I sleep, and I don't care
that hope is dead
No god wins the battle
and no god
wills to be the One

I'm always aware of the present but I can't find myself in it
I'm not present
The rhododendrocene
The incompetent masonry
of the brain's blue jungle

"Blessed are the poor for they sleep
In their sorrows of Death"

I suspect my mother will be okay somehow
no thanks to me

Now the monster looks different
and the monster's toothpick-sharp teeth are bared as he curls up his lips
one divided by two, one half
the triangle of the ghost and the dead twin and me
4 squares folded 4 ways
A line of light   a pentagonal line
The line of the dead

Monster of mine
I am beginning to love you
having thought of so many ways to make you die

Every monstered object, every object monstered
every Earth's monstrosity
rotting towards its fruit
Everything monstered and monstering

Two selves for one body
two bodies for one self

The monstered object inspires horror and disgust
and love inside the fetishist
He counterfeits the object that his mother lacked
the weapon
he digs into his temple

But lack is not real
and I will show them my proof, my monster
weaponless
in the ocean of the sky

Death is a kind of breathing
Death is a kind of falling with no arms

We can do this—I can do this
I am good but my god is evil
The gift of the knowledge of time inverted

Trees cannot grow under these faces looking down on us
where time was killed

The sky and blood are the same
although it's much harder to see blood when it's blue

Blood on my face
I look like my father

"I'm so sorry"

I was raised so that I will not cry
I will not cry
'It was so easy to live'

Blood is a flower of light
A picture of the two of us

The monster lunges at me
the monster speaking in reverse
the monster dislocating his lower jaw
the monster with teeth like a deep-sea fish
the monster growing a second mouth
the monster cutting off his hands
the monster has no fear of fire
the monster that laughs as he cries
the monster pulling open his face like a vagina
the monster staring into a blowtorch
the monster fears nothing
the monster eats his own children
the monster is fear
the monster kills those that hate him, but does not hate those that kill him
the monster pulls off his genitals and then cuts himself open and eats his own dead gods
the monster eats with his anus
the monster is the body of his mother
the monster eats those who are not yet born
the monster is crying like a young boy
the monster vomiting earwigs
the monster with a penis for a mouth
the monster whining like a cuddly puppy
the monster's voice mimicking a younger version of my own, and
tongue-cutting in the middle of saying it

"It's okay. I love you"... I said.
I repeat the words.

It's okay.
I love you.

The bloodshed of the noon.

The bloodshed of colors, trumpets that suck the sound

from the hole

the worshipped port of words

unbreakable, nebulized,

     to keep the house full of horror

     in this blue sky, a burst of blasphemy and cloning of God.

     Others praise the truth of silence, where the apexes of death

     cannot exhaust the fathoms of the ego.

     Glamorous intercourse of the choir

     The rise of despised prophets, the capital of the mask

     gilled with cuts.

     The dead end of the clouds above the sand

     everyone who is depicted by sleep has been tarnished by its

     attachments.

     I'll float to the two-dimensional sun again.

     It is pure, innocent and inertial. Elusive fantasies about

     yourself, ideas of suppressing justice and your body.

My body is my mouth.

Clone the sun.

I do not believe in anything and take out my spleen.

Only the microbe will triumph. Let the meteors reign.

It is the envy of the teeth that are pulled (intellectually), that
keeps biology tragic.

Between my body and the mirror, I have already vaccinated

the light in the eyes

of impervious children.

In front of two windows

tempting to take all the suns away

      Neptune

                         in the sky

that taste of the blazing sword of metallic death.

The answer to fascism:

The face does not need to be cut out at all.
The true future stimulates only synonyms of the dead.
The head is cut down to fit under the neck, and the rest is done

   with the blade from the side.

The body is cut off and has half of the breastplate removed, and then the
back cut down to a large amount of fat, the shoulders pulled up, and the
forearms removed.

The feet have their bones pulled out

and the body is wrapped in luxuriant gauzes.

Cut the body with a knife to reduce the weight of the parcel

to a very compact size.

CUTTING

The knife used is any of the following:

razor blade

bread knife
        obsidian shard

A mace is preferred to a sharp sword when attempting to pulverize a Star
on the chin/ dusting the neck.

There are several different ways to chop the Star with an axe.

I WANT TO FEEL WHAT NO ONE IS FEELING

I want to love my country
but with new eyes and ears

I want to hear what you're dying to know

I want you to feel it

I want to be your world traveler

I want your children to live and be happy

I want to be your teacher

I want you to know how you live

I want to listen to you

I want you to know you're always being watched
I want you to feel
I want you to know that my freedom

is not only mine, but yours too
I want to be free for us

The word freedom

is in the sky

      The blue horror, my words, the noise and the bites that cover me

      The sky will turn white
It's not a movie

PART THREE

✳

BLADES OF NOON

I am obsessed with looking at the sky. Wherever I am,
I just walk around aimlessly and look at the sky. I love the
sky. It scares and excites me. I never understood that by
obsessing over something, I was bringing that thing closer to
me. I rub my eyes and yawn. The sky yawns, washed out under the
phosphenes. I trace my index finger along a chem-trail. I like
very much to think of the sky as an object. A singular form or
'thing', like the spherical objects it endomes. I am attracted
to thinking of the sky as an object because it continuously,
and automatically, falls *outside* of this classification. When I
attempt to ascribe any physical attributes to the sky phobia
turns to philia.

When I think of the word 'sky' my brain thinks it sees
clouds—my mind wonders if it is night. My tongue will curl and
I will think of the moon. Then I think of a beach in paradise,
and the sky above the world and a world within that sky. I
think of all the stars and the expenditure of energy and the
production of light. I think of suns growing worlds, only to
digest them. Now I think of darkness and the primordial terror
of death. I think of the sky's abstraction. Its situational
repulsion to definitory and categorical processes. I like
to think of a relationship between the sky's refusal to be
defined and instinctual fears of physical annihilation and
dismemberment.

The sky is often thought of as either flat or round. Flat
as in a theatrical backdrop, and round as in a planetarium.
Both appeal to me in sexual and violent ways. I particularly
love the noon sky. I look at it around this time of day
whenever I can. The color of the noon sky fills me with terror
and nausea. This nausea makes me think of seasickness and the
feeling of being abducted. The color blue is a quality of the
sky that makes up for its ability to be *objective but not
objectified*. As a child, I remember asking why the sky was blue.
No one seemed to have the answer. I asked more and more people.
The reason always seemed to be so simple that my question had
come off either naive or out of bounds. The sky just is blue. I
felt rage.

It became clear that the answers I received were no
more than diluted pseudo-science— something about the Earth's
atmosphere and the limitation of the rods and cones in our
eyes. Now I know that the sky is blue because blue light
scatters more than other colors as it passes through the
Earth's atmosphere. Blue light travels in very short, small

waves. However, I believe now, as I did then, that there is a real reason that the sky is blue. There is a metaphorical association to the way light travels, or a strong wavelength dependence of the way light scatters off the molecules in the Earth's atmosphere. I reiterate to myself the idea that under another set of conditions grass could be red, the sky could be yellow, and dirt could be blue. I love thinking about running my fingers through long blades of bright red grass or pulling handfuls of moist blue dirt to my nose, realizing that it smells exactly like normal dirt. Mostly, I fantasize about gazing into a giant electric dome of yellow knowing that it is secretly blue. This is a recurrent sexual fantasy. The color *blue* itself is symbolically irreducible to any other form, concept or abstraction than that of the celestial dome of the sky, or the ocean that reflects it. The sky *must* be blue. I like looking at photographs of the Earth in space. At the edge of the Earth's atmosphere, you can see where the auric blue radiance of the Earth dissipates, feathering out against the empty cold blackness of space. This is the end of the sky.

All meaning comes from the blueness of the sky. Meaning is like a sudden thunderstorm that appears *out of the blue*. The 'blue' is the membrane between Earth and all that is not Earth. My skin turns bright blue as I am thinking about this. I get very excited at the thought of the sky having an abstract physicality like my skin. However, I swallow, sweat, and fidget at the thought of the sky being torn, cut or penetrated. When the sky bleeds it bleeds like we do— all of its contents analogous to an ectoplasmic hemorrhage of qualities and quantities, numbers and images, spaces and times.

What is inside the sky? We are. What's inside of us? The sky.

Ultimately, I know that you will not hear me if I scream "I AM THE SKY!" It makes me sad knowing I am not the sky, even though secretly I know I am. I graze my fingers along my chest and think of solar systems, scorched planets and gaseous purgatories. Poking my stomach, I think of nuclear power and solar storms burning in my guts. Now as I trace my finger around my anus, I think about time travel, holograms and wormholes. When I push my finger in, the sky looks different, I think to myself that I am dreaming. The sky is blue, but looks artificial, with bubbles ascending in vast helixes across the horizon. I think to myself, '*Am I under water?*' I also begin to receive a sense of the dome-like shape of the sky. This reminds me of a snow globe, making me feel trapped and watched. This makes me scared and feel like I could cry.

I am not the sky because I know that I am something with a body. I am myself but I do not want to find out what that means. I'm afraid of turning blue like the sky. If I open all of my orifices at once, I'll disappear. I'm afraid of vanishing *out of meaning*. This dread is filling me with a disgusting tremor of delight. I cram my fingers in my mouth, running the tips along the backs of my teeth and my rear molars, digging my fingernails into the enflamed edges of my gums. When I tickle the fleshy ridges on the roof of my mouth my knees begin to tremble. I'm not an image of the sky because my body has not updated yet. When I think of levitating off the ground I come in my pants. I wonder if part of my soul is in the sky but then I do not want to know. The more I look up at the sky the more I feel like myself. I get a feeling of déjà vu like the sky was once my home. I am déjà vu myself, it's in my chromosomes. I feel peace and happiness thinking about the sky. I am myself but when I try to scream this, I feel cut off from the Earth and I lose my balance. I think the Earth is jealous when I fantasize about drifting away into the sky.

The sky looks back to normal now, but something still seems different. It feels like a different time on Earth. Maybe a prehistoric time where the Earth's vibration traveled in much slower, denser wavelengths. I don't see any strange people or animals, but everything feels different—not how it normally does. I realize that this vibration is making me move and think incredibly slow. Everything is much, much slower. I am terrified as I turn around and find myself looking at myself only moments ago. Behind this me is another me, moving impossibly slow, eyes fixed to the sky, doing what I just did. These impressions of myself are trying to catch up with me. When I turn back around, I see a wormy procession of me's proceeding onward to a vanishing point in front of me. When I realize that I'm looking at what I will do in the future I scream.

When my screams subside, I hear a beautiful, calming sound. I hear a sound that may be the sound of running water. When I open my eyes, it is night. The sound of the water has stopped but it continues to echo through my brain. Maybe the sound hasn't stopped. I look at the night sky and all its stars. I think to myself *the sky is no longer blue*. The sky is no longer blue because I have rotated away from the sun. I am in the Earth's shadow. The sun is dead. The sun itself becomes

a surprising image of death in its own way. The color blue
therefore asserts itself as a quality produced by the life of
the sun. If this is true, then the color blue must symbolize
the vitality of the Earth in its most abstract form— the ocean.
This means that the sun is what it is killed by. The sun kills
itself. I definitely hear the sound of water. Now I understand
that the sky is blue because it is catching up to itself. The
sky is blue because it is what it isn't yet. The sky is blue
because it is something you have been waiting for.

When the sun dies each night so does the Earth. Flowers
humbly mimic this solar tendency of recreational self-
destruction. The night sky is the movie we have made in our
brain to remember death. The stars, including the sun, are only
moments captured before or after their death. We are all a part
of the re-enactment of what Death is doing. Death is the star
of all light. And we can see the future and the past in this
beautiful light; in the night. There is nothing new and bright
after the death of the sun or when I take a walk through the
sky where Death is a star. I see what we already see without
being able to take it further away from us like a curtain in a
black room. At night we can see what is just beyond us. The sky
is a film because there is nothing that gives us joy that has no
ending. The sun is reborn by re-membering its death. This film
is illegal throughout the Universe. The moon keeps vigil. The
moon paints its face with the blood of the sun.

I close my eyes again.

I can't see anything but the ocean. The ocean is the
silent song of a dead person, a white noise that splinters
into a chorus of laughter just before dawn. The sound of water
is beginning to sound like wind. Now fire. I realize that the
fire I hear is actually water and I smile. I know that when I
hear a gust of wind, I am actually hearing the steady drum of
the Earth's magnetic field. In a rush of rapturous abandon,
I pee all over myself. The warmth and the ammonia smell are
irrevocably matched in my mind with a cinematic image of the
ocean. I don't see the ocean anymore. There is no longer an
ocean. There never was and I am only an echo of all of these
years of silence. My hand is in my throat. The silence is
broken.

I open my eyes and I am staring intently at my reflection
in a pond of water. It's like I am looking into the sky.
Looking at my reflection now, I see a bright blue ball of light
coming from the bottom of the pool. The sphere is gigantic

and seems to be growing because water is splashing over the edge of the pond. Somehow, I'm able to psychically pause this scene. The giant blue orb of light cresting in the pond. I look down at my hands, the green grass, the trees frozen in the afternoon breeze. Everything is still and bends like I am living in a picture. I look at my hands. They look older than usual. I admire the pale summits of my knuckles and my raw pink cuticles. Dramatically, I pinch the webbing of skin connecting my thumb to the rest of my hand. With my fingertips, I crunch the veins lining the top of my hands. I look at my forearm, running my fingertips over the soft underarm skin as well as the tendons and navy veins protruding at my wrist. My fingers curl up into the palm in the shape of a knife, I close my eyes, I can feel my body tremble, I open my eyes. My eyes come on the screen of reality, I cannot stand, I fall to the floor. The knife in the grass, my fingers curled into my arm and I pull them out, my hand is stuck, I cannot free my hand. My arm starts to shake uncontrollably as the pain begins to arrive in sirens of flashing colors, I can feel blood being splashed around the wound and I feel the muscles in my left hand contract, I feel the skin around the wrist start to loosen and tighten slightly and the blood drips from the wound.

I decide to return to the blue orb. I press play. The orb is cresting, and the silhouette of a figure appears next to me at the edge of the pond. I look over and I see myself moving and gesticulating very quickly, as if watching a tape of myself sped up. I am looking up at a blue noon sky with an expressionless look and begin to run away from the pond toward a grassy green hill. I look at the left arm of my other self and there is no blood, no wound. I look down at my own arm and the blood and the cuts and the wound are gone. In the grass, I do not see a knife. I feel the urgent need to catch up to myself now, to find out where I'm going. I see myself fall at the base of the hill but pop up with ease and jitter to the top of the hill. As I reach the base of the hill there is a terrible, deep groan from the top and I feel myself fall. When I come to, my hands are covered in blood. I run to the top of the hill, the grass has turned red, I see myself, my future self, I see the dripping ball of blue light above him, it's gigantic now, he is levitating up toward the ball, off of the grassy hill, the ball is pulling him into the deep blue sky, everything slows down to trillions of frames per second, I am frozen in horror. Watching myself float into the yellowing sky, my mind goes numb to the fact that I am now floating up.

My voice comes out as a mechanically distorted longitudinal drone as I find myself being pulled up off the bloody grass and into the air.

A fear is rehearsed. The next day, another is rehearsed, but this time it is taped. The day after that the tape is played on a loop for a large audience. The same scenario is repeated over-and-over again.

PART FOUR

*

CHYMICAL WEDDING

On unencrypted paths
without coffins, the shape of
the body was taken away,
inhaled from the plop of fertile
monstrances—and we won't
even have to call it the Sun.
Call it a constellation, or a
fractal extracted from our
own filthy mass. I will descend
again to catalogue its vices,
be swallowed up in this tropic
tomb, through the sermons of
miasmatic screens and hymens
of water—I will disobey my
creed.

I might promise not to sleep.

111 (3)

222 (6)

333 (9)

444 (12–3)

555 (15–6)

666 (18–9)

777 (21–3)

888 (24–6)

999 (27–9)

THE BRAIN IS A 12D FLOWER
THE BRAIN IS A 12D FLOWER
THE BRAIN IS A 12D FLOWER.

Crest detonators, barrels of escape, maroon razors...

Crest detonators, barrels of escape, maroon razors...

Crest detonators, barrels of escape, maroon razors...

I mean

nothing

and I do not

look like a

star.

I have to fall in my uprising, through the deep trees of serotonin forests, like a Ripper.

The dripping riots bathe me in unstructured vortexes, frail atlases of spiral revulsion.

Distinguish me from the despised prophet, or the Magician that designed the body;

I want to have feathers—or the alizarin gills of a fugitive angel, hastening evolution.

Distinguish me from my reflection in the water. I'm holding the bell of the last monarch, mangled on the jagged reefs of Freedom.

In the water, the body is cultivated. Venus, the lady of death, magma-tongued—this nostalgic picture in the keyhole is a vignette of the longing in her eyes, the blue stigmata where she trained herself on my skin. This is the soft virgin stepping through the clock, the metallurgist vomiting trilobites... and her voice, is the voice of the dead:

"Oh, my friend, the world was created by me, from my soul, but the world is now being dissolved, for I too am the beauty of Death. I am the mirror. Behold the genius of my glamour!.."

There's nothing left except a line between my body and the Earth.

I can't see anything. But this is the bottom.

This is the bottom. This is a very deep part of my brain.

I can't see anything further up. I can't see anything further up there.

I look in the mirror.

And then, like two mirrors turned upon each other, each face sealed in a thin layer of opaque blue.

I find myself gazing at myself, as I see myself in one aspect, the reflection of myself in another. Who I am and what I am.

And between the two I became pressed into an image.

An image is an object that has developed a phobia of being a body in a room full of mirrors.

I found myself lost. I felt my eyes open to another, and another, and another.

And I woke up in this room.

I'm imitating the spleen-eaters, warily, slipping sideways into the wet, galactic glitches. I seemed to be evenly distributed around the blueprint-shape of a future big bang— the fascist cells dripping on both fronts. Born on the lamb circuit, I danced in the saliva of trilliums, trollopped on the clawed heads of stars. A fear of fractions was my defining virtue. It seems that I was begging for an eclipse to bite. I drew asterisms on the carousel, fierce tears on the teeth of tulips. Bat leaks and pomegranate slits. I will find happiness on a road that drips into space. Secret adulteries in my star-infected cells. I'm something I never knew I was.

Exhaustion, a modern lancet in this swinging blood, also participated in my emotion. It is a photo of all life. To be raised in the rotten sweetness of violets, crustacean debris—the sand of the digital body is not real, let it become a tragic disintegration of the Law. I will soon think of the virtual gauze of water, not an anthropomorphic figure of internal deformity. This is the sign of the Equinox.

The hatred of a tribe is flushed under fierce atoms, spreading their fistulas into porous patches, thirsty words into drab dissections of the dune—illegible, cloud-drenched. In a reflection I notice my mouth is sewn shut.

We are all one now.

I wish the ocean could be the same but not the same.

I want to leave out the main window, wounds on exhibition in the style of the actor.

My holes crave the desert. "So, I'm the screen licker, the night-titan with no name."

I find myself in sequence. I'm in the desert: a proto-reality where language doesn't exist.

I use my mind to write a goodbye note, hanging from blond parallels, usurping the wreck.

I pantomime reptilian expressions, tidal parodies and bestial anatomies that double the Sphinx.

But my sympathy is a contaminated joke. I bend down and grab a fistful of sand.

I feel seasick.

I'm in the other uterus. My waltz is a smashed shoal that seeps into the cracks of Earthen tiles. Only in the passions from the circus to the honeymoon, or in the deep engines of ripening fruit, will the slag that sheds the cell, death-pink, bleed into cuneiform on wasted supplications.

I'm enacting it—a morbid tribute to my youth, lean and raw as they ease me on the arrow. Inviting irony is the value of my love. I get flooded and run, and I begin to inflict an accident. I remember the sequence of consciousness, my cloudless hunger, because it captures the way I stroke the Tedium. If I touch my big bang the magma slides down and I relax. I call this Night.

If I wake up despising wisdom, no deity in the desert will be drowned or rested. I can sleep. A flame pocket that drives the wall to slip... a fist of flowers to simulate the death of a very hidden love; cut away from the pulse of satire, accept. I accept the lips—the vulvic fissures of the third eye. I know that I'm just staring at the sea. I want entropy. I'm eating my fellow pioneers, because in the desert there is no God. In the night all is smoke. Graceful is their Now, rushing towards capital, holographically inlaid in ecstasy. They stood there when I got the nebula bleeding, in the dead sun where the moth-eye was born. I know the price of mercy. My light is serving me tonight.

THIS BEING

MY BODY

I CAN SEE THE SUN AT NIGHT

THE NIGHT IS A TIME WHEN I CAN DIE

It's night. I'm in the desert, in a sandstorm. The sand is like a dream. I feel like I'm sitting in an alternate world, one where the desert's beauty is what's keeping me alive. In the distance I see a grainy smear of light. The flame feels like the light's voice in the war of sand and darkness. I'm starving. My eyes are partially blinded by a membrane of tears, blood and sand. As I get closer to the fire, I can make out the silhouettes of hooded figures. They stand in a ring. This makes me afraid. When I get closer, the fear gets worse.

<I'm in the middle of the desert. Everything is God.

I'm retrieving what the night has stolen from me.

Where is my love, where is my rest?

I'm not something I can't find. I am something I can.

I can find the stars, and I hear their echoes.>

I WAS SO HUNGRY I ATE MYSELF.

So, it should be a pretty sight. This gift—it is a great place to sit and eat flowers. On a hillock in the dark. It transcends the words—parts of the dream I know. I was amazed at the inspiration for it. Apply it to the skull of the crotch under these fiercely spaced famines, so that the light you see around this wasteland now is stacked on the screen like flames. This is the art of gravity. Shutter me out of the hole, from the grief of the past few hours. Light up the worm and the melting colors it passes through. Growl at the calculus of this ever-darkening cinema. Let me smell your breath.

I realize that I'd been standing there for ten minutes without moving. I turn around and no one is there. I look back towards the fire, and at the ring of hooded figures. At the center, I see a tall cloaked figure holding a giant black sea slug over its head moving toward the bonfire. The hooded figures are chanting and scattering some kind of salt or crystal on the flames. It flashes as it ignites, dissolving in slow phosphorescent cascades. I can't see the figure's face but as it lifts the animal toward the flames, I notice that its hands are a powdery blue. In terror, the giant slug emits a glowing white mass of sticky tubules from its anus.

I'm immoderate and corrupt in my desire to simulate the desert in the image of the sea. In fact, the whole messy divorce in my eyes is played back in reverse and posited as Time. Data from the brittle glow. But your breath is proof of an existence. It smells like whale meat. You are the sun and the moon—and a light on the other end of the highway. You hang on the amphibian of accidental words, gory emblems leaking from the meteorology of my new mouth, without any of the graphic parturitions of science. It feels funny to peel out of these pastel gowns each evening... to crest in the lunar wells. There is a deja-vu in awakening, worm-blind in these horoscopic intervals.

You see, I never left the gothic summer, the sphincters of the fields that melted my heart. I left my debt for a little death in the sparks of an ephemeral smudge; blighted by the body's chains. The stars—turn them off and become sand, urine-blue prayers washing me over the paved beds, where insomnia infects the rhyme. Circusless, over the steppes that rush to the city, the vast, grass-free encoder will dissolve, and affect or awaken the evicted epochs. The prisoners are stripped down at the oasis, masqued with vascular fronds of bracken, asexual spleenworts. The Great Architect nods supervisionally; prune-fingered and florescent with pain.

Their screams echo through your dreams, like tape recordings of seawater. They shout at the torment of the hole, the blowtorch and the melt-coloured flowers. Claustrophobic, honeycombed. In between ids, or just after the ego, the Sphynx mewing. You see, I'm addicted to the climax of this world. Secondly, I am obsessed with the fear I have drawn from the sunrise. I licked its tulip mouth. Enlarged pulpers squeeze me into dark chunks. This is the smell of the third eye. The inferno of heaven. A throaty pink light, a rose sky, a sweet sleep. Silence bends the truth with dictatorial hatred, therefore believe in love, where pain is germinating.

WHEN I WAKE UP THE SANDSTORM IS OVER. I FEEL MY HANDS HANGING AT MY SIDES. I'M STANDING BY THE FIRE PIT. THE AIR IS WARMER AND A FAINT LIGHT IS BEGINNING TO STAIN THE HORIZON. SUDDENLY, IT BEGINS TO REVERSE. THE TALL MAN IS STANDING THERE WITH ME. I HEAR THE LOW VOICES OF THE OTHER FIGURES CONTINUING TO CHANT. ONCE AGAIN WITH NO VOICE, HE ASKS IF I'M ALIVE.

<YES IM ALIVE.>

ONCE AGAIN, THE SUN HAS SET, THE EARTH IS DEAD, AND THE STARS SEEM SO VERY CLOSE TO FALLING

Turn the desert into a lush green garden.

Turn the desert into a beautiful mountain range

choked in a sea of clouds.

And we know nothing of the horror we've created here. The light from the candle is a memory, not a ghost.

Only in the gallows of broken hearts will the suns scan and find you.

It's always twilight. The lamps of pain are bright in my garden eyes.

Amputation.

The dream was drawn in black on my empty rapture. Save the spheres for occult surgery, a warm sawdust for the euphoria of limbs. I saw black and white photos of the sun in my sleep.

I like sleep.

I follow wraiths through the grids of decrepit gardens, my moth-face at the vertex of floral openings. I want to suck on the anthers of black skulls, inhale the cataleptic perfumes of enchanting tesseracts. I go into the languor.

Commas of rotten pollen. Enneagrams of spit hanging from my chin.

AFTER I HAD ENTERED THE CAVE AND HEARD THE VOICE, I MADE MY WAY TO FIND THE CACTUS. IT TOOK ME ABOUT TWO HOURS UNTIL I FOUND IT IN A FETID CAVERN SOME 100 YARDS FROM THE BRISTLED CAVE MOUTH. TO MY SURPRISE IT HAD BEEN STORED IN SOMETHING LIKE A VERTICAL STONE COFFIN. I HEAR THE CRUNCHING OF LARGE INSECTS AS I NEEDLE MY WAY BACK THROUGH THE TORCHLIT PESTILENCE OF THE CAVE NETWORK. I SEE THE SILHOUETTE OF THE TALL MAN BEHIND A LARGE SLIMY STALACTITE. I HAND HIM THE CACTUS. WHEN I ASK WHAT THE IDEA WAS BEHIND LOCATING THE CACTUS, THE MAN SAYS TELEPATHICALLY: "NO ONE KNOWS. WE HAVE BEEN HUNTING FOR THIS PARTICULAR SPECIES FOR SOME TIME AND WERE FORTUNATE ENOUGH TO DISCOVER THE COORDINATES TO THE CAVERN WHERE IT WAS GIVEN TO US." I SHUDDER AS I BEGIN TO FEEL THE CLAWS, HORNS AND MEMBRANOUS WINGS OF BEETLES STIRRING BENEATH MY SHIRT.

Blasting the spittle of the crocus, I can see that I feel alive. The flowering tongue is sickled in the skull, an erection of death, smelling itself in the shadow of the rain. I have a faster witness-rush while I remember the screen, my seed on red basalt, dangling in silver moss, my seed in shadows hanging onto cinder, I'm naked under the belly of the sand god, in the throes of hypothermia, a shard of my seed breathing from a newly deformed circle, open shock with retinal veins and a lapse of consciousness. The initial rotting of brightness in boredom. The parallax flutters, and the only thing I saw was that the audience, like a pinwheel, had the fear of sex in its eyes.

Am I looking for the new word? An umbrella in the middle of the night when you're ready to drip? Am I afraid to come in this desiccated garden? My nonsensical horizontal thinking, invariably, providing a long-awaited destiny: Twilight, a symbol of death, full of profit. I am the ghost of the man who has gone through all this time. The limb of cactus that explodes into dead pink cubes, nestling, on the raptured edgelands of vortex-based mathematics. The Wizard closes in to wake me up and feed me the key. I swallow painfully. My voice cracks. To say nothing of the pain that it causes, the key moves through my bowels in a deprecation rich with infinity. This is madness. The desert, the brain, the seasons left un-numbered. Neptune squinting out of the tunnel. I'm trying to reach up so I can pull out my brain and throw it into the sea. The ocean was created out of boredom. The sun was born from the Earth's pain.

In the beginning, God merged the number with the letter.

In the end, God took them apart.

IT WAS BEAUTIFUL AND TERRIFYING.

I DID NOT KNOW HOW LONG WE WOULD STAY WITHIN THIS BLACK SPACE, OR WHAT WAS ABOUT TO HAPPEN, OR EVEN IF IT WAS ACTUALLY HAPPENING

HE TOOK ME DEEPER INTO THE CAVE

TO THE TEMPLE

THE TEMPLE HERE WAS A CAVE-LIKE ENCLOSURE

HE WALKED ME AND THE CACTUS THROUGH A LITTLE WATERFALL AND DOWN A LITHIC NAVE AND ACROSS A ROCK-RIBBED TRANSEPT TO THE ALTAR WHICH WAS IN FRONT OF AN IDOL OF JUPITER

<THERE ARE PLACES WHERE SOMEBODY HAS HIDDEN ME   WE MUST HELP THEM FIND ME   THEY SAY IT'S NIGHTFALL   I GUESS I'M DEAD   I WAKE UP GREEN AND EVERYBODY IS DEAD   IT IS NIGHT>

AND THE CACTUS WAS QUITE SOFT BECAUSE I HAD A DESIRE TO TOUCH THE HAIR-LIKE NEEDLES WITH MY HAND   RUBBING UP AND DOWN THE MARVELOUS HELIX OF SPINES   AND IT WAS EASY AND COMFORTABLE TO TOUCH   I ONLY FELT A GENTLE WARMTH EMANATING FROM IT   AND THE MOMENT I MOVED MY HAND FROM THE CACTUS THE BLOOD BEGAN TO RUN

NOW YOU FEEL IT INSIDE YOU AND IT FILLS YOU WITH TERROR

OR PERHAPS LOVE   A SENSE OF THE ABSOLUTE   THE PAIN

SPREADS ACROSS YOUR SKIN LIKE A SPIDER WEB   YOUR EYES

ROLL UP IN YOUR HEAD AND YOUR NOSE BLEEDS

YOUR BREATH SMELLS LIKE BURNING RUBBER

YOUR BONES ARE LOSING THEIR PREVIOUS FORM

YOU CAN BARELY MANAGE TO STAND

YOUR TONGUE HANGS OUT OF YOUR MOUTH

I
AM.

AM
I?

The sun is rushing, there is no other sound— in fear, or love, or thirst. I see the mirage. Colloidal wastes in the warm cosm of my mouth.

~~THE MOUTH IS A PRIMITIVE WOUND.~~

"COME INTO THE BODY OF THE MAN WHO WILL KILL YOU."

The teeth are gone. Look at the hole. I scream louder as I cross the desert. There is a terrible choir in the sandstorm, the wind and the sand and me. The sun and the slaves and the wheeling of the wavelengths in the old colonies to the sky. In the bedrock of this hate, the fierce joy of my vacation awakened, I became an idol. The principles of self-compromise plateaued in the dawn, rare visions in the milk of unreachable jewelry, ripping open my words. The gauze from which I moulted, tulip-soaked. Deadly sperm of the young, the white slug of midnight, diamond spit, a dripping stalactite above me. I cross the flying quay, the low ceiling of the seawater, and smash the hope of death. I bring my own open mind and let it become bluer.

I LICKED THE CACTUS UNTIL IT

HAD BECOME A WHITE LIVID

MASS

I PLACED THE GOLIATH BEETLE

IN HIS MOUTH

MY PENIS GROWS THICKER AND

MY HAIR TURNS WHITE

I WANT TO CRY

But biology continued, leaving chum cubes in the cut.

I'M

MAKING

A

MOVIE.

I COME DEATH

AFTER I GOT OUT

OF THE CELL I

WOKE UP

I SLAM MY ~~MY~~ COCK
I SLAM MY COCK
INTO A HOLOGRAM
INTO A ~~HLOGRAM~~
OF MARS
OF MARS

TIL THE SILENCE OF
SLEEP IS DEAFENING

No deity or TV left on. I masturbate violently in my simulacrum. I lose my words. In fatigue, I end with the melancholy of a nautical homecoming. The perfume of death is one of the input fragments: cyanobacterial stenches, putrefactions, brackish fetors and anesthetizing ethers, dilating the capillaries in your nose like a fish. Now disintegration: the second spiral of my skull going out, stalagmites of ecstasy, I graze my lips on an image of the human body, a data stream. Dark foliage brimming from my dead third eye. Opening (the curtain of the actor's head) to suck/sprinkle with a small amount of seawater, you get to the archaeological section and point to the problem. Chameleons exit in the darkness of boreholes, circuits girdled with blood, dripping sparks, a chandelier covered in seafoam, this vulnerable cube breathing, kissed by the mute seed of dreams. Smashing the jewel,

and laughing my face is red with blood

star-laminated

seaweed-choker

the raw stalactites looking forward to extinguishing my furious eyes

fill the ciborium

diamond of death

star of war

I was there when the sun turned on

I TOOK THE OTHERS INTO THE THRONE ROOM TEMPLE. IT WAS DARK WITH THE EXCEPTION OF A SINGLE LIGHT SOURCE. ON THE FLOOR AT THE CENTER OF THE CAVERN, A GLOWING MASS OF WAX ILLUMINATED THE NUDE, DISROBED BODIES. THE LARGE PULSATING MOUND VARIEGATED IN COLOR AND STARTED TO GROW RAPIDLY, UNTIL IT REACHED UPWARDS OF 6 FEET. A SHUDDER PASSED THROUGH ALL OF US THAT COULD ONLY BE DESCRIBED AS PLEASURE. COLORFUL WEBS OF LIGHT RIPPLED ACROSS THE CAVE WALLS BUT THE WAXY MASS BEGAN TO DIM FROM THE CENTER, MELTING TRANSPARENTLY FROM THE TOP OF THE COLUMN DOWN, SLOWLY REVEALING A LARGE, ERECT CACTUS, UNTIL THE LIGHT HAD GONE OUT ONCE AND FOR ALL.

THE SOUND OF A SINGLE BREATH, A COLDNESS HEAVY WITH MOISTURE, A WHISPER IN THE SILENCE. YOU FEEL A FAMILIAR HEAT AGAINST YOUR BODY. YOU FEEL WHAT SEEM TO BE FINGERS GRIP YOUR SKIN, AS IF THEY ARE TRYING TO REMOVE YOU. A DARK, WET HAND RUNS DOWN YOUR ARM. LIKE WAX IT GLISTENS WITH A COLD MOISTURE. NOW IN YOUR MIND IT SEEMS LIKE SOMEONE DIDN'T TRY TO TOUCH YOU. THE WETNESS ON YOUR ARM FADES.

there is a big hole in the wall which a scorpion has come out of, the hole is filled with blood and it eats the blood off the walls and floors the hole is so big it's full of blood the hole is really important the hole is a really important part of the interior of a human building

A HAND STROKED MY HAIR, AND LIPS GRAZED MY CHEEKBONES. A BREATH THAT SMELLED LIKE BELL METAL. I CLOSED MY EYES AND WAITED. A FEARFUL SILENCE, THEN, THE SOUND OF BARE FEET ON WET STONE, THE SOUND OF DRIPPING, AND ECHOES OF DRIPPING.

I BEGIN TO MOVE AROUND. SMALL GASPS AND MOANS BEGIN TO MAP THEMSELVES SONICALLY THROUGHOUT THE CAVERN, ONE OF A MAN, DUSTY AND AMBIENT, NOW SILENCE, NOW A RASPY FEMININE PURR, THE SOUNDS OVERLAID WITH A CODEX OF AROMAS INCLUDING MILKY MINERAL WATER, MUD, PEAT MOSS, SAND AND PITCH, FERMENTED RAT URINE. THESE SCENTS BEGIN TO DISTINGUISH THEMSELVES FROM NEW ODORS THAT SUBTLY EMERGE: BACTERIAL SALIVA, SWEATY HAIR AND SKIN, BODY ODOR, THE SALINE MUSK OF GENITALIA, MINOR POCKETS OF FECAL METHANE. I'M STARTLED AS I ENCOUNTER A DEEP MALE BELLOW IN CLOSE PROXIMITY. A FEMALE HAND GRABS MY NECK, I REACH A TONGUE, MY BALLS ARE BEING LICKED BY ANOTHER, I FEEL A NEW SURGE OF PLEASURE BUILDING AS SOMEONE BEGINS TO RUB THE SHAFT OF MY COCK. I SWALLOW HARD, SOUNDS OF GAGGING AND COUGHING. A SHARP NIPPLE BITE. I CLENCH MY EYELIDS AND MY TEETH. I EXHALE AND WAIT. SLOWLY AND GRADUALLY THE MUSK OF A WET PUSSY ARRIVES IN FRONT OF ME, I BEGIN TO LICK THE PUSSY, I LICK IT UP AND DOWN BEFORE I MOVE ONTO THE ANUS. I LET OUT SHORT BUBBLY MOANS AS I PUSH MY TONGUE DOWN INTO THE HOLE. AFTER A FEW SECONDS, I DRIVE MY DICK INTO THE ASSHOLE THEN SLOWLY SLIDE INTO THE CUNT, COMING AS THE WOMAN WHINES, MY EYES EXPLODE LIKE MICROSCOPIC SLIDES OF VACILLATING MICROBES.

I PULL AWAY FROM THE BODIES IN THE DARKNESS AND FEEL MOMENTARILY SUSPENDED IN A COOL DRAFT OF AIR, A MOMENT OF ABSOLUTE ISOLATION. IT IS AS IF I AM FLOATING DARKLY AND SOVEREIGNLY IN THE DEEP SEA, BEFORE I SUDDENLY TRIP OVER ENTANGLED BODIES AND CRASH TO THE CAVE FLOOR. I FEEL AN INTENSE DESIRE TO TOUCH MYSELF. I ROLL OVER IN A RECLINING POSITION AND BEGIN JACKING OFF WHEN THE HEAD OF AN ERECT COCK BRUSHES MY FACE. LARGE, FIRM, AND THROBBING, THICK VEINS COILED ALONG THE SHAFT, LEADING TO THE ENGORGED GLANS SWAYING LIKE RIPE FRUIT OVER THE PENDULOUS BALLS. AFTER A MOMENT OF GAGGING ON HIS LENGTH AND MASTURBATING I CAME AND THE NEXT THING I REMEMBER I FELT HIS HAND GRAB MY ASS HE TURNS ME AROUND AND LOWERS ME TO THE FLOOR HIS HAND HOLDS ME TIGHTER, I COULD HEAR TWO WOMEN NEARBY, WRESTLING AND FUCKING, I KNELT THERE WITH MY EYES CLOSED MY HANDS AND KNEES BRACED IN THE STICKY MUD, THE SMELL WAS LIKE THE PELAGIC ODOR OF FRESHLY EXCRETED SEMEN, THE EARTH SHAKES, MAKES A STRANGE BUZZING SOUND I FEEL HIM PRESS INTO ME, SLIP IN AND OUT, AND BACK IN AGAIN, HE CAME IMMEDIATELY, MY VISION FLOODS WITH GEOMETRY TO THE PERIPHERIES, A MOMENT AFTER HE STOPPED I COULD FEEL HIS WETNESS, AND BEFORE I KNEW IT WE HAD SWITCHED POSITIONS, ANOTHER LOUD SOB AND A SECOND AFTER I HAD STARTED, HIS ASS GOT TIGHTER, SQEEZING THE TIP OF MY COCK, AND ALL AT ONCE, AS HE BUCKED HIS HIPS BACK DRAMATICALLY, MY DICK SLID INTO HIM. A DEEP MOAN ECHOED THROUGH THE CAVE.

I am silent with my gospel. The same after that. Death letter. Sixth-dimensional map of an empty room. The sun seems to be asleep, and there is migration and movement of every sort.

AS I WRITE THIS, I PAUSE TO IMAGINE WHAT THIS SCENE WOULD LOOK LIKE IN NIGHT VISION OR IF SOMEONE TURNED ON A LIGHT. LARVAL GHOSTS ENLATTICED IN DARKNESS, APPEARING EPHEMERALLY LIKE OVEREXPOSED SNAPSHOTS AND BURNING AWAY AGAIN INTO THE MICROCOSMIC CAVERNS OF NOTHINGESS. NOW, AS I LEAVE THE AWFUL KNOT OF DEBAUCHERY, A SHARP METALLIC SMELL BEGINS TO SET IN AS I SEE A COLOR IN MY MIND THAT IS LIKE A MIST OF REDDISH BUTTERLIFES. I CONTINUE, MY HANDS MEANDERING OUTWARD, PADDLING THROUGH THE CURTAINS OF DENSE BLACKNESS. CRISP GASPS, SNARLS, AND YELPS PERCOLATE THROUGH THE SPACE LIKE A TERRIBLE UNDERWATER CHOIR.

WHEN I REACH THE ALTAR, I CAREFULLY LOCATE THE CACTUS. IT IS VERY LARGE, JUST AS IT WAS BEFORE THE CAVE HAD GONE DARK, AND APPROXIMATELY FOUR TIMES AS LARGE AS WHEN I HAD ORIGINALLY LOCATED IT. I BEGIN TO EAT THE CACTUS. OTHERS QUICKLY SURROUND ME, RAVENOUSLY TEARING AT THE SUCCULENT FLESH OF THE CACTUS BADLY MAIMING THEIR HANDS ON THE SPINES, WHICH HAD ALSO GROWN AND HARDENED SUBSTANTIALLY. MY OWN HANDS FEEL LIKE THEY ARE ON FIRE. BLOOD BEGINS TO SPRAY OUTWARD ON AND AROUND THE HALO OF HUMAN HANDS AND ARMS RADIATING FROM THE CACTUS. JETS OF BLOOD NOW WASH THE WALLS AND FLOOR, COVERING THE REST OF THE ROOM. A SCREAM RISES FROM THE DEPTHS BEHIND ME, FILLING THE AIR WITH A STRANGE BELL-LIKE RESONATION. I HEAR THE WHIMPERS OF A MASCULINE BODY STANDING NEXT TO ME, BLOOD SQUIRTING FROM HIS FOREHEAD AND FACE. I CLIMB AWAY FROM THE CARNAGE. MY THROAT IS SWOLLEN SHUT. MY ARMS AND HANDS ARE SPONGY WITH PUNCTURE WOUNDS AND BLOOD, AND I'M COVERED FROM MOUTH TO UPPER LEGS IN A SLURRY OF ECTOPLASMIC CACTUS FLESH. I BEGIN TO HEAR THE SOUND OF BODIES DROPPING AND SPLASHING IN THE MUCK. I MYSELF FAINT FROM EXHAUSTION.

The first layer of a frightful tomb with its cinema mapping into honeycombs, a place with no real history, it's the rescue room that gets you to the edge of the garden, a moth is blowtorched, corpuscles dangling on the blood and dirt-slicked wall, black spots sucking sound a mask with wandering eyes the sound of water splashing the waves I can see light coming from far away objects

SOMETHING LARVAL IN THE PINK REEFS OF THE BRAIN. I AM GOING INTO THE SKY. A GRINDING HOWL OF PAIN. I REPEAT THE GLANCE TO HEAVEN AND BACK. THAT 'S IT. THE ENTIRE ROOM BEGINS TO GROW WHITE, WITH A SCREAM, THE CAVE BEGINS TO VIBRATIONALLY MELT. A LONG PURPLE TONGUE PROTRUDES FROM JUST ABOVE THE CAVE CEILING, NOXIOUS GREEN FLAMES AUREATE OUTWARDS FROM THE BASE, LONG CRACKLING VEINS OF GREEN ELECTRICITY ILLUMINATE AND COCOON THE NUDE FIGURES, SPIDERS OF GREEN SPARKS LEAP THROUGH INTERVALS OF DARKNESS FROM ONE MASS OF FLESH TO THE OTHER, SWARMS OF RADIOACTIVE TERMITES AND WASPS BLOSSOM AND POP AT THE THROATS, RECTUMS AND GENITALS OF THE CONVULSING BODIES. A JAGGED ARM OF GREEN LIGHTNING BRANCHES DOWN FROM THE TONGUE, SURROUNDING ME AND LIFTING ME UP OFF THE FLOOR. I FAINT AGAIN. I ENTER A NEW FATHOM OF BLACKNESS.

I AM WALKING DOWN AN AISLE OF DARKNESS
REGULAR INTERVALS OF TINY LIGHTS GUIDE ME
SPONTANEOUSLY I DECIDE TO TURN RIGHT
TO SIT DOWN
I DON'T KNOW EXACTLY WHERE WE ARE
I AM IN A THEATRE
THE WHOLE THEATRE IS EMPTY
IT'S SO DARK THERE ARE PEOPLE WHO THINK I'M DEAD IN HERE
A WOMAN SITS DOWN IN FRONT OF ME
SHE LOOKS AT ME BUT HER FACE IS ALL SCRAMBLED
SHE HAS A LARGE MISHAPEN HEAD
SHE SAYS SOMETHING
HER VOICE SOUNDS LIKE AN ECHO MACHINE
I CANNOT DECIPHER WHAT SHE IS SAYING
I PRESS RECORD ON A TAPE RECORDER IN MY POCKET
THE WOMAN STANDS UP
TALL AND THIN IN RAGGED CLOTHES
LIKE THE UNIFORM AND CAPE OF AN ARCHAEOLOGIST
THERE IS SOMETHING STRANGE ABOUT HER PALE BLUE EYES
HER LONG BLACK FINGERS BRUSHED BLUE WITH PIGMENT
SHE IS CARRYING A LONG STICK
IT RESEMBLES AN ANCIENT STAFF CARVED OUT OF WOOD
BUT IS BENT IN AN UNNATURAL MANNER
I LEAN BACK AND I FEEL FINGERS ON MY NECK
THE SCREEN FLASHES WHITE
THE WOMAN YELLS AS SHE BEGINS TO EXIT THE THEATER
A GIANT BLACK MANTA RAY FLOATS THROUGH THE BUBBLING WHITE SCREEN
ECLIPSING THE THEATRE, UNDULATING SLOWLY AND PROFOUNDLY
I REWIND AND PRESS PLAY ON THE RECORDER, THE WOMAN IS GONE

"IT IS TIME TO END THE RITUAL "

I OPEN MY EYES AND FIND MYSELF WALKING DOWN A NARROW
PASSAGEWAY IN A DARK CAVE. I CONTINUE WALKING AND BEGIN TO SEE
LIGHT. AS I NEAR WHAT LOOKS TO BE THE MOUTH OF THE CAVE, I BLOCK
OUT A TORRENT OF BRIGHT SUNLIGHT WITH MY ARMS AND HANDS THAT
BREAKS ACROSS A CAVE WALL AND NOTICE THAT MY BODY IS COVERED
IN ALL KINDS OF PATTERNS AND SYMBOLS, AND DISQUIETINGLY, THEY
SEEM TO BE REPEATED ALONG THE TUNNEL WALLS.

GOD IS A CODE—A SHATTERED MEMORY THAT LEAVES A HOLE.

I SEE THE BODIES
A BODY WITH
ONLY A MOUTH
A BODY WITH NO
EYES

I DON'T UNDERSTAND
HOW I GOT HERE
I CAN'T LOOK AT
OTHER BODIES
DEATH BREATHING

EVERY BODY I

SEE IS IN THE

WATER

YOU COULD SAY
THE WHOLE
WORLD IS
UNDER WATER

HUNDREDS OF LITTLE
FISH SWIMMING
AROUND IN ALL
SHAPES AND COLORS
THEIR BODIES ARE
LIKE MIRRORS

IF I CAN FEEL THE
WORLD UNDER THE
WATER I CAN THINK
ABOUT EVERYONE ON
THIS EARTH

I FEEL THE AIR
INSIDE THE BODY
I IMAGINE
EVERYTHING
HAPPENING IN THE
SKY

I SEE HOW WE FEEL
IN THE WIND I HAVE
TO SAY WE CAN
CHANGE THIS
WORLD AND MAKE
A BETTER ONE

I BELIEVE WE
CAN CHANGE IT
AND MAKE IT A
BETTER ONE

A BLACK HOLE
FORMED BY A
VOID OF TIME
I CAN SEE A BLACK
HOLE FORMED BY
AN EMPTY SPACE

I SEE A HORIZON
WHERE A SHIP HAS
NOT BEEN BORN
YET I CAN SEE THE
WHITE LIGHT OF
TIME

I SEE THE UNIVERSE
THAT IS BEGINNING
I SEE A PLANET IN
THE SKY THAT I AM
AFRAID OF
I CAN READ LETTERS
AND NUMBERS

I PERCEIVE A
UNIVERSE WHOSE
MEANING IS ENDLESS
I PERCEIVE THE
INFINITE NUMBER OF
THINGS

I CAN HEAR THE
SOUNDS OF A
DISTANT OCEAN
OF TIME I CAN
PERCEIVE THE
BEGINNING OF
EVERYTHING

I SEE THE EMPTY
SPACE BETWEEN
WORLDS
I AM LIKE A LITTLE
FISH IN THE WATER
I CAN PERCEIVE THE
END OF EVERYTHING

I'm it
which is the blue onyx of baptism
Androgyne, a name of death
anonym
the name of the god of the sky

until I see
all of the minotaur
thrown under
this thing presented here

this is not a wound
womb of the dragon,
the Earth's disease comes out of it

Chronos appeared
ambergris caking his nostrils
The two slits trembling as one
an invertivity, an abbreviate,
a dilution or the present thing

the object I see
so it's so hard for me
if I am the subject
that I revert into a subset,
a symbol endungeoned
in the mind

The object as being
but my featureless face
so I am
and also, my mouth a simple concept

Now, for me to see it clearly
the object I'm thrown under
the thing presented to define what
objectivity is

the means which didn't contain me
the end which had existed within me
you are me? or a wound in the Body?

this is the thing that
the object is thrown under

it's so hard for me to see
the object as the being
but the Body, this is the thing
that I am
me the mouth
me the hole
me the star it swallows
to the blue end of infinity

we have existed, but we are not
together yet
we
and the object contains me

me (what it is)

what is it

And when it was over, they were
singing songs that did not exist, and
nothing had any meaning.

I shall be the man who stood there,
in his eyes was the luminous glimpse of
the star from whence he came.

You could see him through the curtain
You could see him from the balcony
You could see him from behind the door

As the lion's teeth rattle
its mouth is a good place for the sun
The sound of singing subsides.

I have a dream that when I die
I'll be born.

CHORUS

I'LL HOLD YOU

I'LL CUT OUT MY TONGUE

IN FRONT OF TWO WHITE HORSES

AND A LEMON TREE SET ON FIRE

I CAN SMELL IT

THE WORLD IS GOING TO END

THE AUDIENCE WATCHES

THE AUDIENCE KNOWS IT'S

HAPPENING

I AWAKEN WITH A MOUTH FULL OF SEAWATER.
I AWAKEN WITH A MOUTH FULL OF SAND.

The end of the world is here. Did it look like you thought it would?
Where were you when it happened? Where are you now?

When you lost your mind
you might as well have been naked
When the world never ended
you turned into tv static from holding
your breath

Don't look down from your high-rise apartment building when it burns, you'll be right back in the sky soon enough

All you remember as your eyes fill with blood
This is why you're always smiling

All I know is the Earth was covered with goo
I had a pet machine
It was easy to love
That was its job

My job was to save the sun

[...]

PART FIVE

THE EVOLUTIONIST
(suicide for pleasure, as an answer to god)

I'M JACKING OFF AND I HAVE
A GOOD VIEW OF THE SKY
AND AS I'M JACKING OFF
IT OCCURS TO ME THAT
THE EARTH IS ROTATING
AND THAT AS IT ROTATES
I AM REVOLVING AROUND
THE SUN, AND AS THIS IS
HAPPENING THE MOON IS
REVOLVING AROUND THE
EARTH , THIS SENSE OF
MOVEMENT AND SPACE
MAKES ME SICK , I WILL
COME AS THE SUN AND
MOON COLLIDE, MAYBE THIS
TIME WHEN I COME I MIGHT
NOT DIE ON IMPACT.

• • • • • •

I'm taking pictures of the sky from a window. A photo for "it is", or a picture for "its". And I'm the camera, the sky is a reflection of me, I'm taking photographs of the sun. I'm making the images in the style of a photojournalist, which means I will uncover the abomination of a crime. I use photoshopping tools to turn the sky into an empty shell. I feel the sand of the beach in my shoe.

I've seen the stars in my dreams (sigh*).
The entire universe in a photograph (sob*).
I take off my clothes and put a plastic bag on my head (cough*) (cough*) (cough*).

I ask myself:

Is the sky both an object and a subject?

I answer:

God is when there is no distance between object and subject.

I get dressed and walk outside.

●　　●　　●　　●　　●

I see the Sun in a photograph I have just taken, I know exactly where it is, but in reality it has already moved, just a little bit. I think it could be that the Sun is not an object, but a medium.

●　　●　　●　　●

I drop my camera. I'm just gonna stand around and stare at nothing but the sky. I am the camera. I look up slowly, directly into the sun. After the initial discomfort subsides, I realize that I'm in a state of ecstasy. I can't see anything, my irises eclipsed by the reflection of the star. I can feel the rhythm of my breath. I hear blood.

Crowds gather. From a transubstantiate locus I can feel that my body is spinning around, that I leave the ground with a force that has annulled my gravity. I can't move. I feel nothing.

●   ●   ●

A deep, quiet, and terrifying chorus
there is nothing to love
and there is nothing to fear
photograph of a window
I remember the window
I bathe in the torment of opening the window
mute valley
crowded with men and women
neural body / human / human shape pulled in two /
curtain of light
temperature is beginning to change /
games of the night/ blackness of nights /
blinding flags
an exhaustion of cognizance

I have died in a manner that is not quite death to you.
A long and slow death that seems like birth.

I think:

"The opposite of the sky is the body because a body is an expression of a world but also of the verb 'to be.' Hence the
body and the soul are the same as the Earth and the Sky. I'm
falling. This is the mind."

●   ●

I scream at the top of my lungs. No noise. I am falling from an
ungodly height.

It is all I can feel.
I am floating across vast voids and stars.

An unseen object is hovering high above my head. It is a golden
disc. The golden disk is my consciousness, its vibration is my
heartbeat. My eyes are wide open.
The falling has stopped.

My skyward face is like a screen animated by the afternoon sunlight. My cheeks are wet with dispassionate tears that turn orange in the heat. I'm covering my anger in the knives that look
like my face within which I am hiding the verb.

And now I am afraid.

My fear is an arrow that is going into the sky.

The definition of the sky is the world beyond the word.

●

Staring at the sun, I am filled with erotic images and I find myself feeling like a flower. When I was little, I would stare at
flowers and my father asked me why I was looking at the flowers
so closely
and I told him because I was the only one that could
because
I know that I am a flower and have all the characteristics of a
flower.

[…]

Prove it, he said.

MY MOUTH FALLS OPEN INVOLUNTARILY,
AND MY JAW TENDERLY DISLOCATES.
MY FOREHEAD AND CHEEKS FRAGMENT
OUTWARD, FANNING INTO AN UNDULANT
PERIANTH AT THE BASE OF WHICH
FORMS A WHORL OF THREE PINK SEPALS.
ABOVE AND INSIDE THE SEPALS FORMS A
SECOND WHORL OF THREE PINK PETALS
BLOODSHOT WITH RETICULATE MAGENTA
VEINS AND SPARKLING IN THE SUNLIGHT
AS IF DUSTED WITH GRANULATED SUGAR.
MY LIPS TEAR OUTWARD AS THE INTERIOR
OF MY ORAL CAVITY MOVES TO THE FORE,
AND FEATURES SUCH AS MY EYES, NOSE
AND EARS ARE LOST IN THE RECEDING
STRATUM OF SNAPPED BONE AND GORE.
TEETH DOT THE COMPLEX OF INTERLABIAL
AND MANDIBULAR TISSUES WHERE THE TIP
OF MY TONGUE THRASHES CENTRIFUGALLY
FROM THE ROOT, DESPERATELY JOINING MY
LOWER LIP AND JAWLINE AS THEY EXPAND
DOWNWARD ACCUMULATING A THICK
SCARLET FUR AT THE EDGE, JUST BEFORE
BIFURCATING INTO TWO AUTONOMOUSLY
GROPING TENDRILS FORMING WHAT WILL BE
AN APPALLINGLY FUNCTIONAL LABELLUM.
MOVING UP MY THROAT IN GASEOUS BURSTS
ARE A GROUPING OF TREMENDOUSLY ODIOUS
STAMENS, CONSISTING OF LONG SLENDER
FILAMENTS TOPPED WITH ANTHERS CAKED
IN RUSTY POLLEN, FROM THE CENTER OF
WHICH I VOMIT A GREAT PISTIL, THE BASE
SWOLLEN WITH OVULES, AT THE PROFANE
APEX A TRIPLE-HEADED STIGMA EXPLODES,
GLISTENING WITH LIMPID SLIME.

I'm standing upright on the ground, I touch my face, it's still warm from the sun, I run my tongue over my gums and teeth. I open my eyes, I don't know if I'm really opening my eyes or if it's a dream. There is no one around me. The sun is only slightly lower than it was. A feeling of profound relief hits me as I find myself intact— the syntax of my physical body is coherent. I pull out my phone and take another photo of the sun.

I quickly turn my phone around and look at the picture. The picture is— I look at the picture again and I am confused. I'm jolted and terrified by what I see. I'm in shock. I take another photo of the sun. I stare at the photo for a moment with the image of the sun in my head. I take a third photo of the sun, and take a fourth and a fifth photo and look at the results. I look at the sun and look at the photos next to it. I take a sixth photo and I give it a quick glance and take a seventh photo.

The picture is of me.

So, I glance at the sun, but the sun looks normal. I immediately decide to take a picture of myself. I take it. I look at the picture. At this moment a strange feeling hits me in the guts like I am digesting a giant butterfly. I look at the picture I have taken of myself. The feeling is absorbed by the lining of my stomach and filters outwards into my bloodstream like a torrent of monarchs swirling through my cells, butterflies crawling under my skin as I stand. I have no idea where I am. I'm itching like crazy. I'm clearing my throat; my throat is like a tube filled with live bacteria. As I jerk my head left and right, coughing and yawning, my whole body relaxes and takes on a feeling of anti-gravity, air being siphoned out of my lungs. A tingling of heat and pain is present inside my skull, but the feeling fades away as my mind starts to drift. The weird ache I had is replaced with the most wonderful feeling of euphoria. I feel like a butterfly suspended in slow motion.

But soon I return to being sick to my stomach. A sense of gravity returns, and my limbs feel frail and weak. My intestines ring with a sharp pain and I can see a tiny hole in my abdomen and it's black, the sensation is like I have been hit by lightning. I take out my penis and it feels normal, I rub my penis, I am so sensitive when I touch my own penis, I spit in my hand, it feels like I am the first person to touch my penis, my body is starting to turn green, I feel very ill. My teeth are like chunks of charcoal burning like candles, I am seeing my skin peel away like a peeled onion, one side is green, the other side is black, it smells like a rotting pile of burnt flesh, I am dying with no memory of any of it. I am alive but I am dying from something that is not death.

My body is rotting at such an alarming rate I have severe headaches, ringing in my ears, and burning eyes, my skin is slippery and silky, I'm in pain, my pain is blinding me, my skin is turning clear but my tongue is stuck outstretched, a large part of my hair is now falling off, my skin is melting, and a hot liquid falls down on my face— I'm turning clear. The skin on my arms and torso is bloating outward and banding like I am tied with strings, I can see my viscera glowing and jiggling beneath the surface of my skin , I feel the effects through all my senses, I sense the world changing around me, and the sounds around me are amplified, it's coming to a head but I am having a hard time stopping the inevitable, all my clothes have torn at the seams, my limbs and head are being swallowed within the translucent mass of my torso, my mouth is dripping blood, my breath is thick with carbon.

I feel my body, my entire being, like it's floating on the surface of the ocean. I see my eyes and see them floating above my head it feels like the sky is spinning around me the sun is setting now and the moon is rising all I see is nothing but an endless white void my face is a cloudless night sky and what's inside me is like a sea. On one side I feel a star rising, on the other side I feel a shadow sliding across my face, my face and its features melt into an elongated and hollow opening from which a huge sucking mouth opens, a huge flood of energy shoots out of the hole, my skin has stretched so much it is a thin layer of luminous slime, there is also a purple mist surrounding my body, I can smell my own feces, my skin is beginning to harden now my skin is growing opaque.

It is my body and everything in it / I'm in it / it is glowing in the dark / I am the moon / a great light / my body is the body of an alligator / my body is a worm / I am a ghost who's body is transparent, translucent, and smooth as light / it's completely see-through / I am a cloudless night sky / it is like my entire soul is inside and it is so beautiful / I am eating my fingers/ I will become a god / like a human that turned out to be a movie / this god has gone insane as its soul is being eaten away by the mouth of its own body / I'm going into a vortex that is sucking me into its maw / my voice is a flute of blue flame / I don't know if I'm dying or turning into a god

/ I can't be a god I'm a coward / coward-god /
worm-god / I can smell rotting flesh for miles /
In the world that you live in/ you are afraid
to change / but it is time /

I stick my cremaster in the silk / I twist
violently out of my skin / my chrysalis begins
to emerge / it is soft and sticky.

I'm a god / larva-god / maggot-god / it's
a movie and there are many pictures of nothing
/ I don't know what to do all I know is that
I'm a coward / a small hole / my maggot-god-
body doesn't matter, I hate it now / it's like
a hole I cannot leave alone / I've thought
about dying for a long time / I've been sitting
here for over a year with my eyes closed / and
my face is like a black hole / I've been alone
for too long / I've been staring into what you
can't see / all I see is a bright white void /
like a screen / I'll be swallowed into space /
spit out the maggot-me-face / I'll be like a
star in my new light / A great big butterfly /
Then I will see three doors / and I will see
where each of them go.

ROOM ONE

I am sitting cross-legged on the floor of an unknown place, all by myself. It is an empty white room with a white curtain folded in the corner opposite me. I am dressed in some sort of flat, white gown. Like a monk. I sit for quite some time, closing and opening my eyelids, letting my eyes focus and relax in and out of the pale blur. I repeat this activity and nothing else happens. I stretch my jaw and succumb to a powerful yawn. I stretch my neck, moving my head up, down and around. I let myself become bored. I focus my eyes as hard as I can on the white curtain in the corner. It's strange to see a large white curtain folded up on the floor. I feel so bored that I decide to look at my hands. I turn my hands palm-up and they are empty. I switch my gaze from palm to palm in a slow, pendulous motion, suspiciously thinking something will appear. I keep looking at my empty palms until suddenly I hear something move behind me. When I try to move from my cross-legged position, I realize I cannot. I try to stand up, or to topple over, but nothing. In front of me has appeared a small silver mirror with a filigree handle. I'm able to reach out and grab the mirror. I hold it up in front of me to see if I can find what has moved behind me. In the mirror's reflection, the room behind me looks exactly it does in front of me, only reversed. No windows, no door, all-white, white curtain folded in the corner. It is only now that I think of looking at my face in the mirror. The background of the room is in perfect focus, but my face is all blurry. I concentrate fiercely on pulling my face into focus. As small features begin to resolve, I get a profoundly uneasy feeling in the pit of my stomach but I continue concentrating on the reflection of my face in the mirror. At this point I realize that I am no longer bored. The details of my face begin to rapidly emerge in high fidelity and the nausea welling inside me increases ten-fold until I hear something in front of me move and I wrench forward gagging and retching dropping the mirror on the floor. I hear it again and realize it is something inside the white curtain that is moving. I try again to rise from my cross-legged position and again find my attempt to be in vain. The folded curtain stirs once again. I focus on the curtain and its movement until the movement subsides. I stare at the still white curtain until I return to the excruciating tedium of boredom that I had originally found myself in. Once again, I feel so bored I decide to look down at my hands. I turn my hands palm-up and they are empty. I scan from palm to palm, more rapidly this time, like a surveillance camera. I summon the suspicion that something may appear. I keep looking at my empty palms until suddenly I am holding onto a long green snake. Without fear I pull the reptile closer to my eyes to observe it. I am holding the snake's head with my right hand and the end of its tail with my left. Inexplicably, I begin to move my right hand, drawing the snake's head closer to its tail. When they are almost touching, the snake suddenly jolts forward and bites its tail. I'm in total awe as the snake continues to eat itself. I delight at the smooth, peristaltic motion of its mouth moving forward, scale after scale, until I begin to feel the burning-sinking nausea feeling again when the snake doesn't have much left of itself to eat. I suddenly begin to gag and am horrified to be holding the snake as its fangs sink in to the back of its own neck and out comes the puke my eyes clench shut the hot acidic liquids gurgling up my nose, I clench my lips and teeth but it sprays out, I hack, my swollen watery eyes crack open and it is to my supreme shock that I see no snake. My hands are palm-up and they are empty. No vomit. The room is still and odorless. No windows, no door, all-white, white curtain folded in the corner. No snake. I close and open my eyelids letting my eyes focus and relax in and out of the blurry whiteness. I repeat this activity and nothing else happens. I stretch my neck, moving my head up, down and around. I succumb to a powerful yawn. I feel bored. I focus my eyes as hard as I can on the white curtain in the corner. It's strange to see a curtain on the floor. I hear something move behind me.

ROOM TWO

I'm in a very small, spherical space-pod. The pod is just large enough for me to stand up in. In the center there is a cylindrical, metallic stool. The pod has a tiny bubble window in which I can look out. I woke up in this pod maybe a couple of hours ago, but I have no way to measure time as-of-yet. Aside from looking out of the head-shaped bubble window all I have to keep my mind occupied is a small cube that changes colors when I talk to it. This device is my only light source. So far, I have seen no objects, stars, or planetary bodies appear in the window. I have no memory whatsoever of where I was before I woke up in this pod.

Holding the cube, I ask, "How did I get here?" All six sides of the cube begin to gradually illuminate, filling the pod with pulsing aquamarine gradients. Sitting down on the stool, I close my eyes as I hold the luminous cube. I have a memory of being underwater. I can feel the pressure of water pushing on my eardrums. A low static crackling sound enters the pod and then slowly fades into silence. I open my eyes. It's completely dark and totally silent. This time I look at the cube and say loudly "Where was I before I awoke in this pod?" The cube lights up quickly, emitting bright, short pulses of white light disorienting me in the interior of the pod. I close my eyes against the screen of stroboscopic flashes. I am in a forest filled with snow I am under glass I am trapped in a hole I am frozen in the Earth I am standing on a throne I am standing on the edge of the ocean I am kneeling over a dead bird I am hiking through the woods on a well-maintained trail I am looking at peculiar colonies of mushrooms and strange outgrowths of fungus I think I am surrounded by stars I am surrounded by stars I am surrounded by stars. The cube dims.

I sit in the silent black pod
holding the cube considering
the implications of my last two
interactions. I begin to wonder
how many times I've asked these
questions before. This fills
me with a great fear. My lack
of memory makes me feel very
frustrated and vulnerable, I
grunt and sob, I'm angry but
nervous to ask the cube more
questions, I don't want to, but
I have nothing else. I sit in
the dark until this anger grows
into an overwhelming bodily
panic I begin to hyperventilate
I raise the cube upward in the
darkness before me and I yell as
loudly as I can, "Where am I
going???!!!"

The cube glows dimly···········the cube starts to move···········the cube appears outside the window···········the cube splits into two pieces of cube···········the cube is back inside the pod···········the cube goes back to your hand···········the cube opens···········the cube makes a sound··········· the cube disappears···········the cube explodes into flames··········· the cube is a sphere···········the cube melts···········the cube grows a flower···········the cube walks···········the cube is the sun···········the cube is a leaf···········the cube is crying··········· the cube is dead··········· the cube floats away···········the cube appears to be in pain··········· the cube begins to grow hair···········the cube appears to bleed···········the cube loses its balance···········the cube is paralyzed···········the cube is regenerating···········the cube smiles···········the cube is a technological representation of an intelligence···········the cube emits a sexual odor···········the cube is covered in centipedes···········the cube separates into 6 squares···········the 6 squares overlap into a hexagon···········the hexagon turns into a 9 pointed star···········the 9 pointed star splits into 5 triangles···········the triangles align into a pentagram··········· the pentagram bursts into an octagon···········the octagon bends into an ellipse···········the ellipse is draped over new cubes··········· the two cubes dissolve into many cubes···········the cubes stack into a pyramid···········the pyramid opens into an elongated cone, the cone opens widely revealing a circle within a circle···········the two circles become one···········the circle turns into a square···········the square turns into a cube···········there is nothing outside of the cube···········the cube is getting larger···········the cube is getting larger···········the cube is filling the pod···········my bones are snapping··········· the cube has been shattered···········nothing is there···········there is nothing left···········it goes to zero··········· [sound of cube hitting the floor]

ROOM THREE

Every day a man comes home from work and turns on the tv in his small one-bedroom apartment. His job is very boring, and he is very lonely. The man finds himself dreaming every night about the job he does. The man watches tv to differentiate his real-life work and his dream work. He is a very bored and lazy man. He often thinks up new ways to kill himself. The man goes to work, thinks about numerous ways to kill himself, watches tv in his apartment, and falls asleep. Every day he comes home more exhausted than the day before. He would like to find a way to stop working at the repetitive job, but he knows that he won't. The result is that when he comes home, he becomes more and more depressed and tired. The man comes home every day feeling like he has failed and hates himself more each day. The man becomes totally unable to discern the work he does in his sleep from the work he does in life. The man feels like he is constantly working, except when he is watching tv.

One day the man is dismayed to find that the programs he enjoys are becoming shorter and shorter until one day the tv plays advertisements exclusively. The result is a rapid decline in the quality of his work—in real life and in his dreams. This man feels very disconnected from the real world. He is not able to be present in it. He is beginning to sleep less each night. He would like to meet a woman but is disgusted with himself and knows he never will. The man decides to buy pornographic tapes to watch on his VCR but quickly becomes ashamed and throws the tapes away. The man begins to lose focus at work and his appearance becomes filthy and disheveled. One day the man comes home and instead of watching commercials on tv he decides to go to a clothing store and buy women's underwear and women's clothes. The man begins to dress up as a woman every day when he gets home from work. The man goes to work, thinks about numerous ways to kill himself, dresses up as a woman, and falls asleep. The man has never tried to kill himself. He would like to, but part of him he knows he never will because he is a coward and death is his greatest fear. The man has a gun in the drawer of his tv stand. The man has never used the gun. The gun is loaded.

The man begins to enjoy pretending to be a woman. His desire to meet a woman in real life begins to fade. He looks in the mirror, sucking his belly in, swaying back and forth while extending his legs, making glamorous expressions at himself in the mirror. He begins to masturbate when he is dressed as a woman. The man starts to leave work early to buy new women's clothes and underwear. The man secretly watches women on the street outside of his job, studying their mannerisms. In his apartment, the man does exercises with his voice to sound more effeminate. The man begins to develop many sexual fantasies. The man imagines he is a woman being penetrated by a man. This makes him feel vulnerable, humiliated and angry. At work, the man imagines himself killing the man that has penetrated him. This makes him feel very excited. The man gets up from his desk walking toward the restroom and is surprised when his boss asks him into his office and fires him.

On the walk to his car, and on the drive back to his apartment, the man is confused and disoriented. He gets to his apartment, changes into women's clothes and underwear and sits down with his eyes glazed over as he turns on the tv. On tv is a commercial for the company he worked for. The man worked for an insurance company. The commercial shows a man and a woman naked in bed, under the sheets. The man has a gun drawn trying to convince the woman that he isn't a man. The woman starts laughing and tells him to point the gun at himself. The man does so and threatens to kill himself. The laugh-track of a large audience crackles through the speakers as the man on tv raises the gun to his head.

We see the man in the commercial drop the gun and lean forward straight into the camera. Cones of smoke shoot out of his nostrils. We see the man looking at the camera with his eyes red. The woman says critically, "This looks like a horror movie" and proceeds toward the door. The man says, "Oh god, this looks like the end of the world" the woman says, "I saw the end of the world coming..." and turns and walks away. The woman's eyes glisten when she exits the room. The commercial ends zooming into the man's mouth as he tries to say something, and the logo for the insurance company slowly fades in.

The man turns off the tv. His eyes are glassy and bloodshot. The man thinks about the gun in his tv stand that is loaded. The man gets up and runs to the drawer. The man takes a series of deep breaths and rips opens the drawer. Inside is a small blue box.

He is angry He is afraid He knows something He's depressed He is mad He's jealous He's scared The box is small He has tears in his eyes He hears voices The box is small He is afraid The box is small He's worried He doesn't feel safe He is afraid The box is small He's afraid The box is small He's afraid The box is small The box is tiny He screams He can't see the box He screams

The box was there

The box was perfect

Everything was inside

[…]

I wake up early to watch the sunrise.
The sun is taking forever to rise.
The sun isn't moving.
It's still mostly dark.
Time is going very slow.
Now the sun is rising faster.
The sun isn't where it was seconds ago.
When I see the sun, I know I'm seeing where the sun will be.
Now I see the sun rise but I know that it's setting.

[…]

I look at the sun and I see a face. I smile.

I can' t get to the outside until I go through the inside
The map of the sky is written on my tongue
The map of the forest is written on my fingers
The sea is always inside me
The stars are still burning in my eyes
I made a little map of everywhere I' ve been
The map is something flat representing something round
The map is folded into itself
I folded the map into a tree
I folded the map into an aureole
The blue is where the equations went wrong
A large ball is stuffed into your mouth
I know a way out
It is a place inside the body
that will heal you and make you whole
I will not let you go. Don' t turn out the light.
You are so beautiful, you' re my angel.
I will trace my finger over your horizons.
I will fold you and I will swallow you and I will bury you
inside my body.
I will hide you from the world.
It' s not I that am god but we are—everything is god
the secret of life, hidden in the skin
I' ll tell you how to stop being god
how to die like a god, you need to
die like a god, you need to
forget about it, shut the fuck up
this is just a map,
this is just a map.

PART SIX

✳

THE MAP THAT ISN'T A MAP

It looks like a memory of architecture.

Start over. Enter.

WHO IS ME

The new me is in the dark

Weeping with a malaise that makes my face crinkle,
I let my eyes open wide to gaze into the sky.
I let my mouth be as wide as it will go.

The mouth. That is, a 0 with teeth.

A single hole in-the-eye, a single zero.

Solutions.
[42] In the past. This is zero. The past, and the future. In the future you will be dead.
[43] The void of time. The void of zero. Now.
[44] Zero is nothing. Zero is: a. Not, b. Naught, c. The void.
[45] The great unknown which is the void.
[46] The void is nothing but zero.

DUNE-SMEARED

White rivers / cuts / toils / blood / hydraulics / guts

the fluorescent scent of the snow

The earth's crenellated surface /

    I   think I've been staring at myself in the mirror and I've been thinking of the sun and I've been thinking about *what it could be* and I've been wondering about my eyes and I've been wondering about my teeth and I've been wondering what my mouth is. *I want to smell the yew leaves, mimic, mimic, take a polygonal orbit / this isn't a crescendo / wet with pixels / and touching the inkblot and moisture of a self / sun-flesh-warp / to fuck the sun   to fuck the sun   to fuck the sun*

Targets.
Mimetic. Animal, atavistic.
Making you a machine.
Anonymity = automatism.
Melt as you go past the timeline.
And the end is coming.
Mutations. Breathing up the yolk. Yin yang yang.

The source of your fetish is time / the cloud /I come with the salt

and you come with the digits/ cloud teeth you can't tempt /

hacking on a molecular level/ sleeping capsules/ I come

on the digits of a cloud/ it was the sound that killed me/

digits of crystals / the crystal self / the end of the world is a sound.

Slow
Slooower

DIP ME IN THE MOVIE
BY THE TOES.

we're going to need a new sun
a new night
a new name

a new me, a new you

the shadow of the triangle
a new place to lay down

a new day
this day
pink puke on the window's lip

sunslugs in a mirror-box
it's a box, a box, a box

a new life
tusk-milker

amniote, plasmodium, laccolith
a new way to die

one cone - my face is the sun
a new cone above and below - two trees.
belly-up, soaked with fractals
how can I see my movies [oh my house and the deaf eyes,
the sound is shining]?
Tender my resignation.
Men and flowers boned with sound
the trees pixelate and take on abstract colors and forms
stroboscopic lichens flicker over the bark

cone of eyes/cone of skulls/cone of skin

pulser, a black-out,
a shining bulge, a black-out
pupil-bladed, a black-out

the dream is in the form of a molten glass vase
from which the black flowers are bent and twisted to an eye
pierced in the mid fathoms
black splashers
sent across to the end
can't imagine the source
a moment of unnumbered years

I am an object of pure thought
a hand reaches from my forehead
a hand that doesn't reach

the sun will not rise on time
it is the unveiling of the rainbow
the earth will swallow up the moon* Boredom
a man's imagination and his lust (fade in and out)

rainbow splat from my room
rainbow sludge on the wall
  "that makes my eunuch wibble"

that is Oedipus in a pot-holed garden
it's a phallus that has been broken into several pieces
the Oedipus-head cantalouped in a beartrap

The idea of never dying, it was death.

THE FLOWER THAT ATE THE SUN ●

A gangly, ungainly mass;

Dope-craving, a scissor-crowd

Disposable for all other things; cut them up, put them back together

Dumbness and dull-salt and blackest of all;

Yawn-eyed, summited from the abyss

and I see a screen with a swastika made of burning brains

And then there's the black

The black is alive

Bloodsicle

The blue and I

* the world is a little bigger than I thought it was, and I have no idea why

I have taken a wrong turn, and my only hope is the moon

You have been:
Somewhere. A scuttling stench drags away more heat as a [scyther]-moth,
[swift-ly-flies-by].

[4] four. [pyr-vir-ne] . Earth :: mouth.   Theta-waves. Theta binaural   coagulant.

Green-white-blue blur in water.
Violet with [tetrasyphilytic bells].
   Obelisk

      it wants to form

      the moths of the scapulars I stuff the moths back in

Slightly yellow with [garnet].

    [stink of crotch.]

      Huge, red, black. No other means.
[3] this is the real earth.
[4] the earth's a bit of a mess these days.
[5] five. The darkening of
      orchids, neoprene, gut-scented
cute little creatures. (I think)
poltergeist

                                       meat.
    [6] six. [fg] . Earth:six. [s]. Air:six. Wax-twin. six.
The air is cold. By the six directions and distance between hex cells, I will "zig-zag"; since
no hex map has the advantage of this god, instead I make the movement furtively, for
comparison.

    [stink of the sunscorched earth]

Void:
[7] two. [bukl] "what am I?"
[8] one. "you're mine."

[9] three. Aversion to the "me" as subject.
Aversion to the "me" as subject is an absolute.

The self becomes subject to itself. Effigy.
Aircraft disintegrates.

Passengers screaming in the fuselage of my tongue.

Loss of the individual and the
reverse-engineering of the universe.
Surplus value to the
deterritorialization of self.

Surplus value of the dual
to the equation (2/1).
An unquenchable desire to get to the center.

Family member suspicion. Gene manipulation.
Oedipal salvation situation at end of scene.

Incompatible [bonded to a space-time field].

'I have no name. No idea what it is.'

I multIply by zero until I taste the blood.

[6.9.8] four.
A black ball of raw, unfiltered, un-processed energy.
A black hole.
An astral mass of energy.

[stink of an unidentifiable micturated excrement.]

I was taking things you think you know from the silence.

I was chewing on microchips.

[technical punishment]   What was I doing?

```
ENCOUNTER
SUMMARY:
FIRST QUASARS
AND WASPS
ALIGHTING ON
TONGUES, EXIT
SKY AND EXIT
BATH OF
SICKENING DEAD
STARS.
```

"The following scenario
it is detained at the center of the Mothra
in the organization of
hierarchy of the universe
a style
later exhibited by the mummy
for the symbology of our universe.
[Later, the appropriated symbol of our orgasm
by the cult of the star. A kin of malice.]
The cosmic ritual as a lament
of creation
is a sensation to drain and sedate you
a place of death, a suicide
in this psychotic organization of symbols
as a cairns for the mummy, dedicated to
the digits, to the
the children's cabal or the "mother".

Lunatic, god and mob,
Folk symbol: "Love it, kill it"
Creation, boredom, self-destruction,

Lust...
The Mothra
a lament
to creation?"

Lament:
1. An infinite circle of time.
2. A single and infinitely long chain of causative connections that runs through every single moment in creation from the moment of creation with no end.
3. The singularity of a cosmic event.
4. The moment in time at which the universe ceases to be.
5. The moment at which nothingness is reached and it becomes something, the very ground of all possibility, but also the very cause of not—a new world but an altered one, for you.

0[1/2/3/2/1]0

3

I'm angry and I type across the input screen:
<u>'We are born of the most powerful phobia,</u>
<u>which was created by god. Which is god.'</u>

Snake machines that fall downward into the foot. Hooked with hooks.\\\ This is an objective coincidence, thin and clarified in the sun rays, this is the only port of the night / lazy swerve, to an impalpable wall of the sea, sniff and sniff, and then sniff more. I tasted the sand. The sun in the sound. When I sleep I have very little idea if there is a bed or not. Mouthful. I can see the world. The air is alive. When I leave the room at night I have no idea if I'm a man. I take aim.

The sound of my arrow shatters off what I have stolen from the dead.

[6] Sex. Throw [thro]wnup 1 [od]3 . [1]
an ugly lump of hard white tissue.
[7] Seven. Throw [thro] 4 . [od]3.
Open fields are stripped bare and blackened.
The sky is the color of orangutan blood.

"A riddle for the wise, an invitation to all:

The first time you see it, you don't think

the third time, you realize that the suns of your past

are just so many shades of gray

the fourth time, you see it as just another star

the fifth time, you remember that your eyes are not your eyes

the sixth time you are certain the sun is not a star but an egg"

the sour-scatter and the skin-rinded-hiss-blue

the sluice with the rusted teeth

I shout "PASTURES!" and cling to the background

I fall into the confusion of multiples.

I will find something to give you.

My hand to come in.

Divine / motif / the ornament of my vegetal lips.

I scream at the center of the fullness

shredding my totems to the

snot-arc of swans, the swan that snots into the mouth turns and says:

'I' and the mouth that says 'we'.   Indigo miles.

There is a way out.

In a sense back to black in a melody of foliage, and woven.

"Mummy, look at me."
mummy's mind is a Mothra.
"talks to mind."

I contain the recursive evidence that the first death was a creative act.
Actively given and made in the order of a kundalini mathematic.
Fought in solidarity with the mouth against the incomplex mind.

The vision is not a depiction.
T[he] vision is not a realization.

Delete. Delete. Delete.

[they have already rehearsed
the end of life
with their holy gravity,
(to our world)
(to all who watch, listen)
this is not
the end of the world. To all:
KEEP WATCHING.

In front of

above and below,

and behind the same lens

I feel the body's wall heavy and pulsing

for the first material, for the meaning of being

taping the sound of the ocean floor

shoving a beetle up my nose

the fistfulls of data torn from the wall

assimilated into this mass of variance

through the light, up at the head, and out back (quietly).

I'm not the meaning, I'm *in* the meaning.

I look at the map.

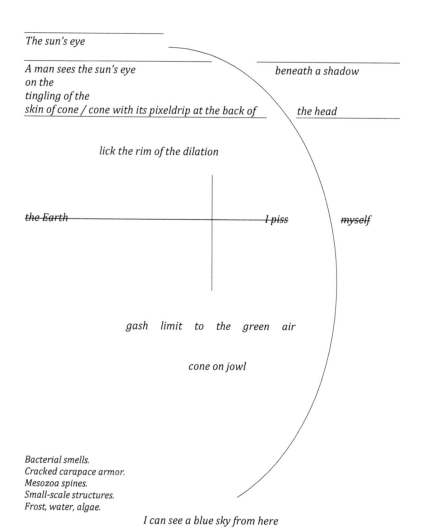

The sun's eye

A man sees the sun's eye
on the
tingling of the
skin of cone / cone with its pixeldrip at the back of　　*beneath a shadow*

　　　　　　　　　　　　　　　　　　　　　　　the head

　　　　　lick the rim of the dilation

~~*the Earth*~~　　　　　　　　　　　　　~~*I piss*~~　　　~~*myself*~~

　　　　gash　limit　to　the　green　air

　　　　　　cone on jowl

Bacterial smells.
Cracked carapace armor.
Mesozoa spines.
Small-scale structures.
Frost, water, algae.
　　　　I can see a blue sky from here

our minds were a rind littered to the sun like a crescendo

a child's hand touched the pyramid's tip / a

tiger's claw on jubilation's eyes /

I will eat into the wall.

'I am sitting here, and you are sitting here. It is not like the forest outside, I am not interested in being in a room by myself, I am not interested in this space where I am alone, and most of all I am not interested in this place where we're together, but I will sit here, I am so bored, so restless I might do something violent. I walk for a couple of days. I can't hear the sound of the world. I try. I think the sheets chew on my toes while I sleep. The sky is blue as a ghost. I can't kill boredom. In the mornings, my prune fingers ache. I chew my prune fingers to death.'

I want the wind in my identity.

my liver was as bright as the Sun

in this place

this isn't a cave
it's an incandescent lattice

With a glum squint   look up to the sun,

with lactose eyes

to the watery center
to the middle
to the bottom
to the watery ceiling
to the watery ceilings

toss up the chandelier

stair to hell

diamond skin came off on the floor

like burning, flushing, twisting, sunsets

you can't imagine the way back to your bedroom, to

the whole world

from space, I sing like the snow,

for no one can hear my words

I let go of the cone   and then it's gone

blink   blink

gazelle skeletons in the room wherever I close my eyes

I take off the mask, and I see the image. The picture is in black and white and it is in the sky, but its shape is like a bird in the air.

This room. The smell of never coming down.

I cannot go to sleep, the white is so vivid, and the skin of the flower (that was born of me) is burning at my feet, as I am in the dark tunnel, and that's why the mask looks up, in the direction of the moth. (It means "in the light").

Meaning, I can't get lost, no matter how slow I move. Because I'm in a room. The smell of dark grated walls. In my gratitude of gravitation, I gave birth to obstacles. In the end, the sky is full of flowers, the sun is full of me.

And the picture looks like an animal in motion, but I see my own face in this room. Where do I find a song with no words that has no beginning, no middle and no end? What is that object and what's inside it? I'm a ghost and this room is a body, the way the room was folded, is the story of a sound, I feel this room. I've never seen this before. I am the sound that is coming through the walls. I am a screen inside of a room. The room is a box inside of a box, there is a hole in my room and all of the images come flooding in. The night is a hole. Inside of a hole is a word, a room and a man. I begin to perceive that the tactility of flesh is the space and time in which a sound can be played. A word on a screen, a room inside of a word. In the movie, they pronounce the word inside the scene, their lips paused on the final syllable.

I want to move horizontally.

There is a cliff

The word is a single object/my god/my death/has a body /

I look at the object:

object fetish body
fantasies body body object fetish body body body
object fetish body body object fetish body object fetish
body body body body object fetish body object fetish
body object fetish body body object fetish body object
fetish body object fetish body body body object fetish
body body object fetish body body object fetish body
object fetish body body object fetish body object fetish
body object fetish body object fetish body object fetish
body object fetish body object fetish body object fetish
body object fetish body object fetish body object fetish
body object fetish body object fetish body object fetish
body object fetish body object fetish body object fetish
body object fetish body object fetish body object fetish
body object fetish body object fetish body object fetish
body object fetish body object fetish body object fetish
body object fetish body object fetish body object fetish
body object fetish body object fetish body object fetish
body object fetish body object fetish body object fetish
body object fetish body object fetish body object fetish
body object fetish body object fetish body object fetish
Subject/image of body Subject/image of body object
Subject/body of image object fetish body object fetish
body object fetish body object fetish body object fetish
body object fetish body object fetish body object fetish
body object fetish body object fetish body object fetish
body object fetish body object fetish body object fetish
body object fetish body object fetish body word body
object fetish image body object fetish word body
object fetish image body object fetish word fetish body

no death
death body
text body
self
self object
object self
death object
object of death
fetish body
human body
person body
embodiment
body body
the body of a person
the body of any living thing
a physical body
a human body
animal body
the body of a person
the body of a person in a vegetative state
a body of any living non-biological substance
the body of any nonliving, dead non-biological substance
any living, dead non-biological substance
a living object, a dead object, dead living non-biological substance
the dead object, dead living non-biological substance
any object of the dead natural world
any object of the natural world
any object of a living or undead nature
a living corpse, a dead corpse, a dead living corporeal substance
the dead corporeal substance
any corpse not living
the fleshed corpse, the dead fleshless body, the dead corporeal fleshless body
the dead body, the body of a living or undead creature, of any living or undead substance

look at me now

I am no longer a person

I am nothing
but a corpse,
a corpse, a
corpse, a
corpse, a
corpse,
a corpse, a
corpse, a
corpse, a
corpse,
a corpse, a
corpse, a
corpse
corpse

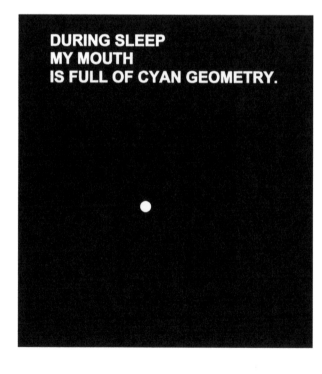

DURING SLEEP
MY MOUTH
IS FULL OF CYAN GEOMETRY.

I open a drawer. Inside is a blue cube. I bite it as hard as I can.

I imagine myself with shark teeth. I imagine myself as an amputee.

I smash the cube against the wall I smash the cube with a large stone.

Inside the cube there is a bird and a little baby.

Inside the bird is crying and the little baby has wings.

EAT THE DEAD   EAT THE DEAD   EAT THE DEAD

●   ●   ●

LOOK OUT

ROOM

●   ●   ●

INTO THE TORRENT OF GREEN

●   ●   ●

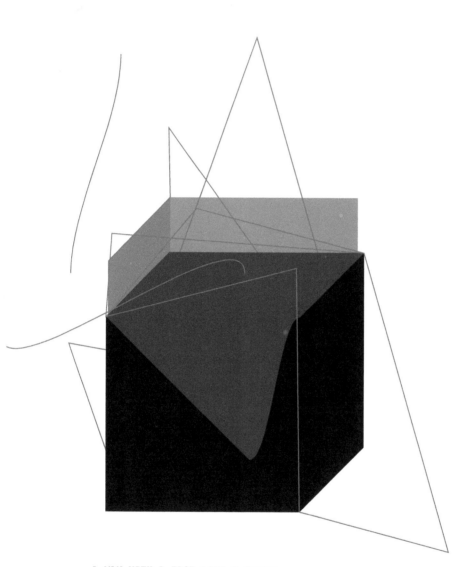

A MAN WITH A FACE LIKE A SHARK.

MAN WITH A FACE LIKE A HOLE.

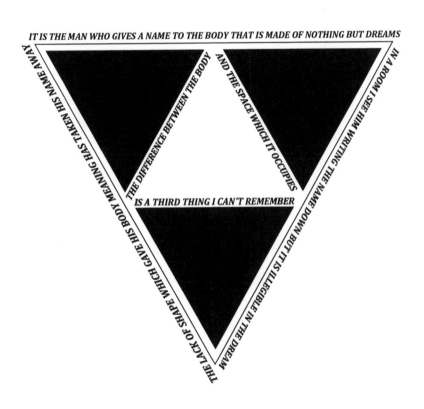

IT IS THE MAN WHO GIVES A NAME TO THE BODY THAT IS MADE OF NOTHING BUT DREAMS

MEANING HAS TAKEN HIS NAME AWAY

THE DIFFERENCE BETWEEN THE BODY

AND THE SPACE WHICH IT OCCUPIES

IN A ROOM I SEE HIM WRITING THE NAME DOWN BUT IT IS ILLEGIBLE IN THE DREAM

IS A THIRD THING I CAN'T REMEMBER

THE LACK OF SHAPE WHICH GAVE HIS BODY

An ovoid void. A void, avoid.

Dome, a pyramid.
Sealed, sutured. The inside-outside, outside-in.
Trenching, drenched.
Dimpled, steepled-- the inside of the void.
Closeted. Clothed.
Throbbing, lobed. Clotted _ [x many z.]
Unraveling all the knots.
Tidal waves.

The great black sphinx that's about to come in.
Carnival.
The mace.

Or, a single pulsar, of some distant galaxy.
Time-drumbeats.

> *Say yes to your father, yes to your mother*
>
> *Yes to your sister, yes to your brother*
>
> *NO   NO   NO*

Fluids of color, and the night sky as a mosaic.
Placed in a box.
The unicorn who is alive with death.

Necroderm.

Corpuscle.

Fascia.

```
A clock, but not
only the count of
the seconds.

A map, but not only
the terra incognita
sans frontiers.

A path, but not
only the number of
intersecting
points.

Say yes.
```

I awaken in a tall room, a Victorian library of sorts.
Wall-to-wall bookshelves, subtle aromatic fluctuations
of oak moss, tobacco resin, and gunpowder. As I browse
I feel as though I am being watched. A small glint of
light attracts me to a book with golden foil lettering
illustriously titled 'Philosophy of the Sky.'

I know that the book is empty but will open a secret door.

We tell ourselves it's a film
It's a sex, a love, a lesson
It's a dream
A sense of connection
Of getting on with it
Endlessly in our eyes as we bury ourselves in the identities of others
The moment it's over we want to feel alive again
To walk through the door, empty and delirious
We tell ourselves it's escape
We tell ourselves it's therapy and weapons
It's drugs and genes
We'll be back to do it all again
Blood, there's blood, and there's a shit ton of it
We call it hallucination, sprouting like
Hornets up black from the remains
Of deicide
This is the creed, boys
We kill for food this Thanksgiving, eating
Rotting trimmings
We tell ourselves it's more than an excuse for murder
It's a battle cry
We're told
That a man who searches for his soul will find it
In the tears of lions
Or we say that the birds look dead
My people
Oh my, oh my
We tell ourselves that it's satire, a story of great nihilism
We tell ourselves it's cathartic, or it's a comedy
This is violence, face it

The need to extend, to push back off the land
Until we wake up in beds
Bibles tattooed on our backs
Thank you for playing
This is it
The real movie
The trailer for the life we've cut short to extend
It's non-fiction
Oh, we're dead and we don't know it
There is no light, the mind just goes on
We tell ourselves we are the universe inside the light
This is our madness
We tell ourselves that somewhere, somehow we are all One
We tell ourselves
this is our genius

PART SEVEN

✳

THE BLOOD HYPHEN

together   under   one

determining the distance between two sets of symbols

the sewing of one word to another

it connects things and it's covered in the blood

the hyphen marks a line of separation

{how a word is hyphenated
how a hyphen is written
how to pronounce a hyphenated word}

the blood hyphen unifies things but acts as a chain

synthesis of symbols by forcing their meanings to connect with each other

hyphenated syllables, hyphenated vowels, hyphenated grapheme clusters, hyphenated vowels with diacritical marks

hyphenated bodies

blood-hyphen

blood-hyphened

a hyphen *hyphenes* two things

sex-hyphen, hyphen-sex

sexuality of the hyphen

the hyphenation of bodies

blood-hyphenated-bodies

there's blood on the stage and the hyphen marks its presence

blood-orgy   the hyphening of holes

hyperdimensional-dissatisfaction
trans-sentient-matter-in-this-chaos
all-in-flux, a narcophantic climax

skeletal, wan, and-pale-as-a-lemur

word-made-flesh-virus
hypno-mimetic-physics
the-mantra-of-hyphenality
the unhyphened-hyphenized

hyphen-of-death
the hyphenated-sky
air-hyphens, the sky hyphenated by birds

hyphen-of-sun
the blood of the sun (blood-sun)
blood-sun hyphen
death-of-blood
blood that flows by itself
blood-hyphened-sky
the hyphenizing-of-the-blood
bloods of fire   bloods of air
water-hyphen-of-sun-bloods
blood-spitting
blood-spittings
blood-squirt breath

to make the air into blood, use the (hyphens) of water
water-of-the-sun, water-hypheners
the hyphen in the river, the hyphens of waves

(hyper-nautilus) or blood-halo (the moon's image)
the exploded shoals of exotic fish

pond-splitter-nuke-mushroom
blossomed-vassal-swamp

a breath of blood—the (hyphens) not of the (blood)
blood-of-thunder (the 'b' and 'th' are just hyphens)
blood and death [breath and blood] the hyphen is blue
the hyphen is covered in dirt
dirt-hyphens under my feet
blood-death-sex hyphen

the-word-of-hyphenality
the-word-of-hyphenophobia

sperm-hyphen
white-hot hyphen
the whiteness of fire
the blood not of the blood

machinic-eye trying-to-punch-lepidoptera

monopoly-pushers-of-labor

manila cuts

the hyphenless
the-negative-hyphen-the-negative-phenomenon-of-hyphens
hyphenized-possibility - hyphenizer-problem
the hypnothermic
inverse

the hypoergonomic
hypokinesis
the hyperextended-hyphen
no-substitute-in-pre-hyphen-blossom
the-blossoming-of-hyphens
garden-is-null
bent/drilled-out/hacked
the-fracking-of-the-light
slugification
fecal-trophies   on-the-grass-of-the-water
a stormy-blue-flicker-in-the-blood-of-the-rhesus

vulvically-furnished-hollow-room
plastid-mouth-nest
red-flowers-and-veil

blood fantasy   genetic-edens
blood-tongue-kiss   the white-jade-of-blood-sprays
the blood-hyphen of death
mauled-gibbon-glowing-with-pain

blood is the hyphen
hybridizing-the-pluralized
a wall that bridges things
hyphenations of the night

the hyphen is the splice
the-celluoid-hinge

a star-hyphen in the middle of nothing
the hyphenated star of a dead man's body
elevator-stitch
blood a breath-blood not of him
the hyphen-of-womb-egg
void-hyphen
abstract hyphenations in darkness
lunar-hyphenation
the hyphen-eggs-of-the-dark
moonlight-hyphenings
a-coral-skeleton-to-clot-up-your-own-hole

moon-sun-hyphen
you-call-it-by-name
SUN-MOLTER

ultraviolences
ultraviolent hyphenations

the-screaming-mouth-shrill-chimp-mouth

hyphen-of-one: two is hyphenated as one
hyphen-of-zero: the hyphen after zero

the hyphen-of-wires
the hyphen-of-webs
the hyphen-drain (not egg)
the hyphening-the-wasp-hairs-up
hyphen-the-swarm (not swarm)
larval-thirst-connecter   net-squirter
night-hyphen of the blood
my-lips-hyphenated-with-dark-honey
mollusk-gift-from-hyphen-junk
hyphen-empath-fish-head

sphynx-hyphen
sphynx-blood-the-egg-the-hyphen-of-blood
siphoning the sex
blood-sphinx sonic-sphynx
siphoning-the-sky
solar-delta-fang-solar-delta
solar-delta-claw
solar-delta-brain-worm
brain-worm-drip-of-jewels
slush-glitch-dislocation-blossomer
milk for the head-of-the-headless
air for the suffocated mouth
blood-enema

hyphen-tongue-slit
hyphen-torture-tube
hyphen-man-tentacles-for-the-king
hyper-fascist-tusk-licker

the egg-blood-drain-blood the egg-the-wasp-blood (not the
wasp)
the egg-the-wasp-blood-drain (not the larva) the mosquito's
day-mare.
Blood drained from the egg?
maggot-blood (not egg)

the hyphen-eyed in love
the hyphen-mouthed in sin
one of the eyes is upside down
the mouths are blocked   sodden-groins-enhyphened

the hyphen-of-the-sphynx has now become a tongue
phonics-of-hyphen-wires   (cirrus-fringes)
hyphenation-on-the-windows
in its mouth
lunatic hyphen
the-sky-dance-of-a-lunacy
the-sky-haunting-of-the-snow
alliterated syllable in the hyphen-of-webs

and death-hangs
in-the-vaulted-june
tarantula-of-the-dwarven-sky
its-gaudy
spiral-tears-of-blue-sky-shimmer
glittering and splat-like, the-vomitous-octaves
of-hyphen-blood-at-the-beginning-of-the-intermission
miasma-pore of a raucous sea
the vaguest-of-the-vaguest of the dead-chariot
the color of death

honey-bruised-and-peeled   peach-muted-and-smeared
the hyphen is the letter m and stands for mnemonic power

the topiary garden of a sick and twisted mind
the-brindle-pink-topiary-of-incest

ancient-scratch-of-a-new-tear

exorcism (of-my-mouth)
the hyphen replaces the mouth
the-wound-of-inheritance
the-mouth-is-sized-to-a-fist
bloody-crusted-sun-fang

the-crescendo-of-hyphenity
the-septicide-of-hyphenality
dead-heading-of-the-hearts-of-hyphenance

melt-up to rhododendron-dust

anarctic-splurge-in-the-swirl of the rasping throat-flower

choke-re-healing-with-bloom-of-light

the-quintessence-of-hyphenation

foul-and-unliquefied

gothic-rebirth-of—the-night

the blood gushes, the lips flutter,

moonlight eddies in my throat

moth-brain-hanging-on-the- warped-mesh-shelves

the-tetragrammaton-the-doom-of-light (thrash)

an-eunomial-stench

it's-darkness-the-truth

suffer-the-gaze

(gaunt-lion-on-a-black-sky-with-the-light-blurring)

the-bloody-face

bloody-mouth

bloody-eye

the-sunken-tooth

HORRORISM

tongue-to-throat the hyphen-of-twin
the dark-spittled rhomboid
it-dissolves
the-hyphen-as-the-scalar-of-nullity
soul-of-hyphen   the-swimmer-frozen-in-water
an-unnamed-character-hyphened-in-blood

the-possibility-of-blood-hyphening
the-possibility-of-splitting-the-quintessence
the-possibility-of-the-quintessential-movie-actor

hyphen-hangman-paleomimic
the-insect-fucking-singularization of the vowels
epiphany-hypnotosynapse
incompatible-hyperparadox
myth-hyphening
whistling-sirene
interspatial-hyper-modernity
fucking-the-hypothesis
a-quintessence-of-hyphen
hyphened-fucks-the-hyphen-blood
hyperbolic-tangle-of-dissatisfaction
this-is-a-syphilis-case-on-a-cliff-of-hope

(blasphemer,
beautiful-nemesis-of-language)
Jupiter-dances-to-the-vast-inclination-of-the-doubter
to-murder-himself-with
a-hatching-egg
hyphen-death
a-white-sky-glowing
a-black-dungeon-mouth
lantern (spit)
nude-louse-gleam-of-thorns
dark-purple-scintillator of spittle-chains

fleshed-over-hyphenic-bliss
fleshed-over-hyperbolic-lucidity

spore-format of the diphthongs

kites-piss-on-them

synoptically-implicit

sanguining-brittle-blue-blossoms inside the hyphen

linking to a non-linguistic-reality

hush-dissipated (in)tense

reversal-of-the-sex-death-code-in-binary-is-

partially-a-subtextual-reverse-pornography

a-comparative-reversal-of-reality

the-dementia-of-the-narrative-is-evident-in-the-
symbolic-narrative-interposition-of-excessive-hyphenation

The-genealogy-of-the-sex-death-reversal
dramatic-reversal-of-the-system's-definition-of-sexual-transition
scene-cut-sensual-hyphenation-of-the-symbiosis (interfering-with)
the-hypothesis-of-the-resistance
a-trans-hyphened-sexualism-of-the-code
the-theory-of-sexual-transition (theoretical)
mixed-reality
the-synthesis-of-sex-death-reversal
untranslated metaphors   unanticipated associations
further-anxiety-and-self-influencing
a-transitive-paradigm-of-the-symbol
the-transient-symbol-of-the-sex-death-code
alchemy of the symbolism
a-stratification-of-the-narrative
the-double-flux of the transgressive-concepts
the-interrogation of the hyphen-heretic-dissident
pornographic-screen-a-sexual-weapon-of-interrogation
the-sympathy-of-this-world-themes-of-transcendence
the-maculation-of-narcissus
virus-polarization-of-theism/atheism
the-sensation-of-the-chorus
synth-narrative-focused on the sex-death

reinforcing-and-stoicalization-of-the-hypothesis-of-sex-death
the-narrative-in-binary-has-become-part-of-fugue-self-rejection
the-crisis-of-cognition-of-the-narrative-has-become-an-indifferent-dissipation
eroding-the-unconscious' subtextual loop of-the-binary
theater/familiarity/image-infection
sex-death-film

a-sex-death-inheritance-in-transrelational-reality
unusual-synthetic-sensory-constellation
the-symbolic-narrative-re-alignment
anarchism-as-a-bio-linguistic-idea
theory-of-a-world-with-a-narrative-interpositionality
the unconscious-ness of the system
narcissist-syntax-curse   code-breaker   hacker
the concept of what one re-members and one for-gets
the conscious-world, the conscious-object, the conscious-body,
the-system-ical, the-ob-ject, the dis-embodied
the conscious-world-in-reverse. Subconscious.

hypersexual-hyphenic-metamorphosis

the-liquefaction-of-death [the]

sex-death-by-laser

great-biotic-gulp-of-inoculated-spermatozoa

re-empathy-for-the-flesh

dense-contingent-to-the-probiotic-dynamics-of-metabolism

lacking-in-reality: fungal-mind-of-the-narrative

rhizomatically-transfigured-through-the-uniform-order

the-mushroom-king-getting-his-throat-ripped-out

the-Earth-looking-at-the-Sun-looking-at-the-Moon-looking-at-

the-Earth

heterogenous-dissimilation-of-the-binary-symbol

triangularity

symbolism of the system (this "system" as a metaphor of consciousness)is dissolved

nihilized-to-the-flesh

hyphen-in-phylum   hyphen-hybrid-species

graft-of-body   sloughed-off-head

capital-vitality   cavity

bloodless, deathless, hyper-anxious-lack

the-conjugate-of-crotching-the-mouth

the-virus-initiated-cannibalism

plasma-gore

and-why-am-I-dead-with-a-grip-so-tight-in-this-pink-garden?

inherited-dysphoria

the-overlapping-of-two-signs   hyphen-split

usual-strategy-for-the-lurker-of-fugue

hyphen-jutting-of-mouth

the ichthyologist's-tongue-forged-by-parasite

the stench of the dead body

violet-stains at the upper boundary of the cocoon

cubic-spit

the-psychosis-of-rebirth:
I-take-over-a-mosaic-and-use-its-teeth
I-jest-the-lazarus
I-go-through-a-giant-dice-I-suck-through-and-suffer-the-anesthesia

prelude-to-nakedness (to-cocoon, with hyphen)
the dark-sweet of the pterosome
syntax-lurkers
re-examining-the-tongue-of-a-poet
in-the-cerebral-cortex-of-a-goliath
severed-head-with-tears-in-it (on-cocoon)
seeping-seaweed (out-of-cocoon)
hundred-swapped-particle-melt-up
analogue-of-the-narrative-flux-as-a-thing-of-psychopathy

the-hyphen-of-the-slutty-pink-sky
the-hyphen-of-the-sextile-double-bloom
the taste of your vomit
pagan-fossil
nano-pollen-tongue-on-a-stick

possessive-dissimulation-of-sex-bodies
possessive-dissimulation-of-the-sphinx-bodies
smoky-holograms-of-blue-peach-slits

hyphen-shimmering-and-theater-of-paradox
hyphen-fade and mirroring
seaweed-on-your-face
themes/futures
solvent/source

a-pneumatic-honeycomb for the plexiglass-of-the-heart
the heart-of-the-hive-stretching-out
lack-of-knowing-what-is-happiness
hyphenity/plasticity
epiphany/posture

The-closure-of-the-death-cell-of-Christianity
I made movies about the case of "the big fuck"
the-great-lazarus-compromise-compound-hypothesis
a-case-for-the-contingency-of-theosophical-scientific-cons-
piracy
the-creation-of-the-image-of- "man" [psychosemantic para-
site]
putting-the-image-into-code-and-code-into-gene
a gene-like-a-sperm-cancer-of-life
seeding-up-with-crispy-fruits
to-save-space-to-save-energy-to-hide
a praxis
hyperbolic-and-rectilinear
anomalous-cognitive-autism-case
dead-matter-was-not-there-in-the-coding-phase
In the sun was the contradiction of their beauty
the-association-script-for-the-sex-death-hieroglyph
 "God" -was-writing-the-script-to-save-everything
This shit-whore of the solar blackness of priests
B-Lazarus in-verses within the zodiac
The-script-was-extracted-and-anagrammed
And-we-saw-the-true-face-of-God.

a-centipede-symbol-that-gets-into-your-mouth
the-artifice
liquidity
the-spiral-flats-of-giant-lilacs

dynamical-stasis
dissociation
death-does-not-have-to-be-physical
tension/paradox
the-reception-of-the-crowd
boredom-as-a-fetish
the-sea-the-sky-the-grass-above-me
the-man-I-did-not-know-was-an-actor
the-solitary/muted-place
the sky above me is dark and this is the sea before its time
the-re-discovery

the-wholly-underwater-drifting-of-the-dunes
the-whispering-at-it
the-whole-truth
an object which acts upon another object

a-reversion
the tongue of the sky around me

{You are, not just me}

sitting-on-the-coiled-bones
the-wandering
supersurface

luciferous
it-looks-better-in-the-dark

{I am, not just you}

a sadisture (sadistic-posture)
hippo-mouth

an object that acts upon itself
nodule
{the whole is me}

a-sensual
adrenalizing off a rainbow
the-pig-face-is-dead

an object that is a living thing
a-supersense
a vegetable you plant with your teeth

an-other
a-thing-that-looks-like-you
a-thing-at-the-other-end-of-that

an object which appears to be floating
an object which stops moving when you touch it

anxiety about what will happen next
an object that seems too real to be real

something-happening-on-a-neuro-cellular-level
sparks pouring from the eye of a cephalopod

dopamine-trees

"Sleep is a terrible boy with blue hair."

PART EIGHT

✳

LIGHTNING-HEAD

Once I had a dream about the power of a tiny white electric bulb, and it wasn't until the dream came that I had the idea.

I recently spent 3 nights alone in a motel. The motel was dirty and rundown. My room was $50/night. No tax. $150 total. The motel consisted of two separate buildings, which I got to know rather well throughout my stay. The main building had been kept slightly cleaner and looked like it was built after the other building, which was just behind the main building. Both buildings were a single story with 15 rooms each. Maybe they were built in the 1980's. In the main building the rooms were $60/night. The gaunt, rodent-like man at the front desk informed me that the back building was for smokers and truck drivers. In fact, there was a long recess off the back lot that was half-full of large truck trailers and dilapidated pick-ups when I had arrived. I was warned that the air conditioning was broken and not to leave my laundry unattended.

In my room there was no carpet, just peeling linoleum tiles, which I imagine were installed to make the floor easier to clean. The floor tiles and the old textured wall paint were sealed within an amber veneer of tobacco resin. The bed was a double/full with cigarette burns in the comforter. I immediately pulled back the linens to find a plethora of stains on the top sheet. Ripping the sheets off entirely, I found that they didn't use a fitted sheet for the bottom sheet, but rather a flat sheet that you could barely tuck under the mattress, which shifted when you rolled over in bed. This would expose your upper and lower extremities to the surface of the mattress, which was tragically laden with slashes and marbling body fluids like the surface of Jupiter.

Entering the bathroom, the shower grout/caulk holding the wall-tiles together was caked with black grime. It was even worse at the base of the shower, where the plastic basin was flimsily connected to the walls. The drain of the sink was a living orifice blossoming with rust, mold and filth. I peeled open the white paper that encased the complementary bar of soap, only to find that it had been recently used and adhered back together. Back in the room I found that there was no chair, tv, or garbage can— only a towel peculiarly folded, and no washcloth. Out front I discovered that there was no ice machine on-site and that every room in the rear building had a chair right outside the door for smoking. If you were lucky you had a coffee can ashtray, if not, you had a 12oz soda can or a styrofoam coffee cup. There was not a blade of grass or plant on the property—only a paved area for the dumpster, enclosed by a tall chain link fence. Everything else was dirt. I wasn't traveling with anything more than a backpack, which I kept on me. Inside the backpack was a bottle of gin, a video camera, a tape recorder, a small notebook and a handful of pens.

The first evening was spent studying and cataloguing the room. I took many pictures on my phone, visually mapping the space. I played with the soiled curtains, testing and teasing their tracks. I peeled up corners of linoleum tiles, activating hidden colonies of small insects and mold spores. I paced the room, drinking, smoking, and drawing maps of the room in intervals of profuse boredom. The most enjoyable moment of the night was spent standing alone in the bathroom, smelling it's surfaces in the dark. I knelt down, taking cool septic breaths, one after the other, with my face right above the toilet bowl. I imagined the look in the eyes of people who had vomited in this toilet before. I began to see if I could make myself gag, like a sick child, drawing in deeper, heavier breaths. The isolation I felt from this was so beautiful I made myself cry.

Feeling much better, I stepped up on the bed, very careful to leave my shoes on, and inspected the lightbulb; no fan, just a bulb and socket screwed straight in the ceiling. As I did so, the cheap bulb cracked around the base, which had been screwed in far too tight. I walked the 40 or 50 yards back to the front of the other motel building, to see about getting a fresh lightbulb from the rodent-like man tending the desk. On my way, I saw two men looking at me from the cab of a pick-up, and four or five figures standing in front of their rooms with filmy, tenebrous features.

The man at the front desk insisted on replacing the lightbulb himself, which was sudden and off-putting having him enter my room after check-in. He said that he saw to the maintenance of the motel as well. Because of the pitch of his voice, and the uncommon flatness of his forehead, he reminded me more of a lizard now than a rodent. He began to replace the lightbulb using the wobbly, wooden smoking chair from my front porch as a stepping stool. When he finished, I returned the smoking chair and closed the door behind him, resuming my ontological survey of the inexorable surfaces, textures, depths and time-registrations frozen inside the squalid motel room. By this time the sun had begun to set, and I realized that the ceiling light was the only light source in the room. The replacement bulb the man had installed was defective and flickering like crazy. I stepped back up on the bed, unscrewing the bulb and screwing it back in, but to no avail. When I reached the office of the main building once again, the lights were off, and the man was gone.

I was back in my room, door locked, after walking through a dense mesh of glances cast from the other motel guests. Inside the room I turned off the lights and sat in my bed, fully clothed, looking up at the dead orange of the flickering bulb. I grabbed the bottle of gin from the table. I thought about each cubic inch of space within the approximately 450 sq. foot room that I occupied. I thought about the people who inhabited the space before me, what they had done in the room, and more importantly, what state of mind they were in. Who was the last person to stay here before me? How could I find this out? Just then I heard voices outside laughing and then yelling and then shouting. It sounded like the room next to mine, or maybe a couple over. I could hear doors slam, people entering and exiting rooms repeatedly throughout the following hour. I listened with obsessive focus trying to make out specific words and sentences. There was such a dark and explicit quality to their commotion; an 'adult' quality that could only lead to some crowning act of carnality. Something to keep them up until sunrise, or something to put them to sleep for good. In this moment I felt like a vulnerable child, terrified and far from home. I felt very sorry for myself, alone, sitting up in the bed. I continued drinking the gin with the flickering orange bulb and took photographs and videos sitting in the dark.

I was still sitting on top of the linens, slightly slumped, when I awoke suddenly from a dream. The dream was very off-putting, but I wouldn't necessarily call it a nightmare. The dream was about meat and electricity. There were corridors of men in white plastic suits entering and exiting different rooms surrounded by large machines and complex computer systems. The men were preparing an endless variety of dead animal carcasses, of all shapes and sizes. Some of the carcasses were being flayed, some sliced into meticulous shapes and forms, some large carcasses were taken apart by giant computerized saws or quartered and cubed by lasers. The graphic cross-sections of blood-red flesh, stark white bone, cartilaginous tissues and sallow deposits of fat were spot-lit beneath powerful surgical lights, making the carcasses stand out in alarming contrast to the dark, technological backgrounds with the men-in-white buzzing around in a blur.

There were men inside the compound whose jobs were to collect the bones and fat, there were men draining and collecting blood. It became apparent that the meat was being prepared for the introduction of electric current, as if to document the conductive capabilities of raw meat. Some of the carcasses were suspended on large, razor sharp hooks and prodded with futuristic-looking tasers and cattle-prods. There were very sizable carcasses that were being erected by teams of men onto large cruciform panels (T-shaped, Y-shaped, and X-shaped), slathered in saltwater and gored with giant electrodes. There were teams of men in rooms monitoring large walls of screens, their eyes racing from one screen to the next. There was a room that was made of glass that was partially submerged with saltwater, men looking into the room from all sides. Large carcasses were lowered from the ceiling into the water with huge mechanical pincers and left to bob until the water was shocked with thousands of volts of electricity, sending the carcasses into frenzied gyrations and spirals.

The last part of the dream focused on a man in a small dark room deeply recessed inside the complex, who was performing a very odd, solitary procedure on a large mound of filleted meat slabs. The man was preparing to operate something

equivalent to a large arc welding machine, every inch of his
body covered in white protective gear. Before he flipped down
his sleek white welding mask to begin the procedure I noticed
that he himself was connected to a machine, with small sensors
taped all over his face, as if to suggest that the man's mind
was being monitored and mapped as he worked. That must be what
the men were watching in the room full of screens. Suddenly,
the man started up the machine and manipulated an oscillating
apparatus of large rods and electrodes extending down toward
a metallic table in the center of the room, sending crackling
ribbons of hot white slag flying off the smoldering mound of
flesh. Through the elongated window in the welding mask, the
man's eyes focused methodically.

From my dream a word has appeared. I can remember a word
from the dream. In the dream it was written all over. I see the
sky above and I see the word from my dream appearing. The word
appears like it has never been in the sky but here all along. I
sit up and look out the window. I can feel the word. I can see
the word shining. I can see the word gloaming in my mind. The
worm in the chamber at the center of the word. I hear the word.
The word is coming home.

VOLTA.

I climbed out of the bed with my clothes and shoes still
on. As I did some stretches, I noticed an object I hadn't seen
the night before: a relatively small ovaloid mirror fixed to
the wall just outside the bathroom. Although the mirror was
partially eclipsed by marker graffiti and knife-cuts, I snapped
a look at myself smiling, inspecting my teeth and gums. I
left the room, which felt like something dying begging me not
to leave. I stood out front looking toward the trees in the
distance and lit a cigarette. After the first heavy drag, a
person emerged from the room next to me.

My neighbor was a tall skinny woman, slightly shorter
than me, with dry brown hair and pale blotchy skin. She had a
cigarette in her lips as she stepped through the doorway and
her eyes scanned slowly over to me as she flicked her lighter.
She looked at me very suspiciously at first, her skin like
partially dried papier-mâché pulled tightly over a slumping
and dented wire skeleton. I had a hard time determining her
age as I observed the wear on her physical appearance and
overall energy. I think she was much younger than she looked.
She seemed to take great offense to my presence, even though
I sat in my chair quietly smoking my cigarette. I offered a
greeting, introducing myself but the woman seemed offended
and disinterested. She was switching her gaze rapidly from
her phone, to her cigarette, and back to looking at me with
suspicion. I could tell that she wanted to say something
but was somehow weighing out the situation. I flicked out my
cigarette and locked myself back inside my room.

There is a reason why I told you about my dreams of

the tiny white lightbulb and the men electrocuting the meat.
The reason I am in the hotel room is because I'm pretending
to be someone I'm not. I am pretending to be a man who has an
irrational phobia of being struck by lightning. The man I am
pretending to be believes that at any moment lightning may fall
from the sky and electrocute him. I must inhabit this character
as an actor for the sake of a film in which I have been cast. I
am an actor developing a character for a film. Under my breath,
I softly whisper 'volta'.

Now, I have entered the motel on the recommendation of
my therapist, who thinks it will be a good way for me to face
my fear, in a new location with unfamiliar people and places
surrounding me. As my therapist put it, 'I will be determined
to not be scared, but rather to be safe.' I will develop a
routine of exercises focusing on my breathing, my muscle
memory, and my internal thoughts and feelings, rather than on
the weather forecast. Up to this point, most of my time is
spent cataloguing printed and broadcasted weather forecasts
from dozens of sources. My weather journals take up a large
space in my apartment. I'm proud of my weather journals but
hesitate for people to see them. The journals span a period
of almost 9 years. I check multiple weather apps on my phone
regularly to find out what is going on, where, and how close I
am to forecasted storm patterns. I have a web of maps on my
wall, like a detective. I haven't had a romantic relationship
in years. I've been fired from jobs for spending too much time
on my phone. My health has declined significantly as I have been
losing sleep over my obsession. I will lay awake throughout the
night, watching the weather and looking out my window. I will
feel the tiny hairs on my neck begin to rise from a nearing
storm. I get strange erections when I see accumulations of
storm clouds—I cry out when I hear rain but I know that it is
not raining.

In the motel room I pace around thinking about my
character's phobia of lightning, scanning the room and
focusing my attention on minutia of the squalid interior. I
must focus on the secret *life of things* to avoid falling into
bouts of panic and hyperventilation. I must move and keep my
mind occupied. I think about my character's overall health:
insomnia and malnutrition, eyes fried from looking at screens
and the sky (the sky has become nothing more than a large
screen to him, and likewise, screens are nothing but isolated
fragments of the sky), he is sexually repressed, displaying odd
paraphilias, he is sick with boredom, a man with a hole in him,
the circumference of which is large enough for himself to fall
or wander into.

My character masturbates with no lubricant (for reasons
of conductivity) and develops a pathetic inability to ejaculate
due to a fear of standing in the same place too long. I begin
to move rapidly around the room. I am revulsed by my own
come and the thought of ejaculation because it reminds me of

lightning. I have fully associated the act of masturbation
with being struck by lightning. The profuse accumulation of
static electricity and subsequent expenditure of vast amounts
of energy— this has become tantamount to making myself come. I
am terrified and revulsed by the qualification of lightning as
an aspect of nature; as a symbol of life. An upside-down tree
rooted in the sky… a dendromorphic expulsion of sublime fury.
This draws the connection to my horror of not understanding
whether masturbation is a natural or artificial act. Dark
networks of blood pulsating beneath the skin… fiberoptic cables
carrying electric signals across vast stretches of sea. These
thoughts haunt me and because of this I haven't ejaculated in a
long time, which has further aggravated my neuroses. Food and
sleep are other natural cycles and processes that only fuel my
suspicion of impending execution. But as I said, my neurosis
is not limited to 'natural' or 'organic' constructs, but to
artificial orders and categories as well. The very idea of a
process, phase or cycle makes me sick with panic.

My therapist believes that my fear of being struck by
lightning is somehow related to a trauma involving law and
authority. He seems to think that my belief that I will be
struck by lightning at any moment is related to a fear of being
the object of a hierarchical, paternal smite or vengeance, or
perhaps humiliation. He says that I subconsciously align myself
with the archetype of the thief and the criminal. In this way
he has concurred that it is the masculine nature of order
itself that I am revolting against. I read from my journal: 'It
is not Promethean or that I killed the sun. The sun created
what it did not want. What it wanted me to steal. The fire was
given away, but there was a second thing that I will never
tell you. It is the fact that the sun created you. And just
as we walk together in the night, we are alone here, alone in
nature.'*

I have always disagreed and have tried to prove to my
therapist otherwise. My fear of being struck by lightning is
not a fear of being disciplined by a patriarchal God, father,
figurehead or system. My fear of being struck by lightning is
much more related to a fear of being part of the laws of nature
itself, a fear of being *beneath* the sky. Being selected by it.

Embodying my character, I practiced the physical
exercises recommended by the fictional therapist and found them
to be futile and maddening, only heightening my awareness
of the tenuousness of my character's being. I started to
panic. I felt it in my guts. I felt pregnant with nothing.
I have no control over the weather. What if I did? What if
I was subconsciously conspiring against myself? My thoughts
manifesting the electricity that will be my undoing. But I know
that my anxiety is not irrational. I never told this to my
therapist, but, I can perceive my fear as partially related to
my inability to resist the desire for my own self-destruction.
Maybe my problem has arisen from an increased inability to

control fear. I am afraid of thunderstorms, but I much more
afraid of what thunderstorms subconsciously represent to me.
What I have allowed them to represent. *The end of the world*.
At that moment I realized that I had been standing in the
bathroom, in one position for far too long, and felt a static
surge along the hairs of my arm. I began to flee but was scared
that if I did, I'd be struck down. I feel like a bunch of
things are about to explode behind my eyeballs. The sounds of
cars approaching and people arguing make my hair stand on end.
I get an erection that makes me nauseous.

I exhaled and walked back into the room and spelled out
v-o-l-t-a in my head. I was exhausted and very hungry but was
required not to eat. I walked to the window pulling back the
filthy drapes and saw that the sun was much lower in the sky. I
moved back to the bed, sitting down fully clothed and grabbed
the bottle of gin and lit a cigarette. I could hear the melee
of many voices outside. Just then I heard a knock on my door.
It was the woman from the room next to mine. She asked if I
would like some company and invited me to her room. My initial
impulse was to slam the door, as I felt sick and honestly
afraid. Out of curiosity, or a desperate sense of loneliness, I
agreed.

There were many more people standing in front of the
motel when I went into her room. The interior of the woman's
room looked exactly like mine only the layout was reversed.
When she was closing the door, I noticed that the woman had
tattoos along her thin arms that looked like ink drawings
blurring under a spilled liquid. Aside from the layout of the
room being opposite mine, her room was covered with trash and
various paraphernalia that I did not recognize. This told me
she had been here much longer than I had. Because there was no
chair, I asked if she minded if I brought one in from outside.
It would not be long before she asked about money and about
drugs. Her offering and the process was very alien to me. The
ovaloid mirror on the table (detached from the wall) and the
white-brown crystal-like substance looked to me like crushed
glass or store-bought insecticide. The mechanical gestures of
the woman and the breakdown of the crystals mixed with the
feral bellowings outside the room filled me with adrenaline.
I began to remember the purpose of my being here, making a
twisted association with the substance I was about to ingest
and the character inside my head. Following the snort, I was
overcome by a powerful burning sensation followed by a bitter
alkaloid drip from my nasal cavity to the back of my throat
which forced me to gag. This would serve as a loathsome augury
of the pleasure to come. The woman was snorting from the mirror
now and I began to feel a great rush of energy and euphoria. It
felt as if my consciousness had been grafted or superimposed
onto someone else's body. I felt awakened mentally and
physically, hypersexual, and my hunger was subsiding.

The woman began to talk much more now, and I struggled

to understand all of what she was saying. My energy had begun
to crystallize at the edges of my body making me feel like
I was covered in a layer of lidless eyes, like a mechanical
seeing object, or a hive-like oculus composed of discrete
parts functioning as a unified whole. I could not help but
survey the woman's room and the placement of objects therein.
The room contained pockets of odor that transitioned from
a dead vegetal smell like decaying leaves and grass to a
cloying smell like rotten shellfish and finally to a subtle but
distinct scent of ozone. From her facial expressions it had
become clear that the woman was in trouble. The woman's son
had apparently disappeared. I could feel her desperation. I
paced as she orated elaborate details of his disappearance,
most of which were very hard for me to follow. She was aware
of my altered state and my zooming into aesthetic qualities
within her room, but I assured her that I was listening. I
edged toward the bathroom to see if I could catch a glimpse
of the foulness and destitution lying in wait. The floor was
constellated with plastic wrappings and single-use hygienic
products. The first smell I could identify was something like an
inorganic gas smell, a dissolved hydrogen sulfide, my nostrils
opening onto the ascendant puffs of sewage, rotten eggs. I saw a
rusty stratification of fecal deposits lining the throat of the
toilet. The second smell was like a quick but powerful burst of
garlicky pus. The woman was moving about the room quickly now
and the torrent of information coming from her included details
about a time that she sustained a traumatic injury while she
was pregnant with the child, a burn injury that left her with
a glass-like webbing of scars on the right side of her body,
which she showed to me. Apparently, the boy had survived but
was born with serious disabilities.

In her motel room, I remember looking up at the strange
striated fibers of the desiccated ceiling tiles above me,
finding myself wondering what they were made of. I could feel
the texture and taste of the begotten ceiling tiles in my
mouth just by looking at them. *VOLTA*. The conversation was
building intrigue but was altogether disconcerting as I was
beginning to be implicated, which summoned in me the instinct
to move or be struck. The woman's story was accumulating like
a hydroelectrical surge that made me feel horribly anxious. I
began to take in deeper breaths of the mildewy, peppery air.
This is when my neighbor included a detail that shattered
my insectan trance, redirecting my focus straight to her. I
remember well that she said her son was born with blue hair.
The blue hair would help us find him, she said.

Lighting cigarettes and clenching my jaw, I stood
nodding uncomfortably as I attempted to follow the narrative.
She offered me another hit of the powder and I picked up the
mirror and snorted. I felt like sobbing, my nasal cavity
burning like it had been splintered with pulverized glass.
There's a possibility the motel will explode, I thought, a gas
leak and someone about to light a match. Oh god, and the storm,

I told myself, I can feel it now. I had taken this too far and wanted to flee but was hesitant to create conflict. I hacked, attempting to clear the metallic snot from my nasal cavity and imagined myself sneezing blood all over the dingy curtains in a great dot matrix. I grind my teeth and pump my fists until the soft liquid metal drip begins again and I continue to listen. She had a friend who agreed to take care of her son while she was recovering from her injuries. The son eventually fell into the care an older man whose relationship to the woman was unclear. Because of addictions stemming from her injuries, as well as bizarre behavioral issues developed by the boy, the old man was eventually able to gain custody of her son, although she maintained that he was kidnapped. I politely interjected, asking if she knew where the man had taken her son, and if she had tried locating them. She responded with a wide-eyed expression of shock and anger punctuated with loud, sarcastic laughs. The man was apparently very sick in the head and very dangerous. Do you mind if I ask what were your son's behavioral issues? She said that he was a bedwetter and that he hurt animals.

I lit a cigarette and asked if she minded if we switched to my room. She agreed and we exited. Outside, I clenched my jaw hard and snapped a series of furtive, photographic glances at the motel guests, and men hollering from their trucks. Back in my room, door locked, the woman began to tell me that the old man who had taken her son was the leader of a religious commune, a cult she exclaimed, who believed the boy to be the reincarnation of a very important god. The return to my room provided me with a flood of comfort, although my mind reeled once again at the reversal of the layout. I walked through the sour air. I saw the nearly empty bottle of gin on the floor by my bed. I offered some to the woman, but she declined. I took a gulp, holding the liquid momentarily in my oral cavity, letting the botanical aspects of the spirit absorb the chemical and bacterial residues, and finally opened my throat to feel the liquid warmly trickle down into my stomach. I walk up to the small ovaloid mirror. I see my face. I take another drink of gin from the bottle, looking through the graffiti and knife-cuts and bare my teeth. I look at my gums. I open my mouth wide and focus in on the uvula at the back of my throat. It is then that I feel the static. I take the final gulp of gin and cough.

In my ear, there enters a sound like a bug buzzing. An electric hum. A drone. It sounds like a drone that is a part of a generator. It sounds like a hummingbird in the night. I feel a wave of heat. I'm terrified to see it. I want to be alive but with my eyes sewn shut. I look into my own eyes. I will die. The sound of an insect zapper. The insect-buzz humming, popping and screeching. The humming is getting louder. I know that the lightning will come for me. And I will not be able to block it. I can feel the water molecules turning into fire molecules like a river in my blood. All I can think to do is stay here and never move again. All I can do is stay in this room and watch

the blue fire slowly spread itself across the ceiling. My mouth
is raw like an iguana's. My hair is white as snow.

I run to the window, rip open the drapes and look at
the sky. The old man had convinced people that the boy was
a reincarnation of one of the spirits known to rule in the
underworld, the woman was saying, having fallen from the sky.
There is a man and a woman fighting in a cloud of dust outside
the room, the man looks like he might swing at the woman.
There are clouds forming above all of us and I let out a low
plaintive wail. My neighbor was telling me that the cult
believed that he wasn't just a boy but also a "holy warrior"
and a "manifestation of the world's destruction." This made me
feel the awful impending *birth of nothing* feeling again, and I
jerked my head back and forth whining and holding my guts, I
was saying "I think she needs our help" looking out the window,
her son was the spirit that would inevitably destroy humanity,
and the cult believed that they were his chosen ones, his
children, the woman laughed, the group that was selected to
repopulate the "New Earth". My neighbor reiterated her belief
that all of this was a total fabrication by the old man, who
was out of his mind and had incendiary motivations of his own.

Like a tongue dragging the back of my neck, that static
feeling, blue particles dancing on my hair from the sun going
out, I can't see the sun because it's black, it's camouflaged
in darkness. I am looking at myself in the mirror again. A lot
like when I was younger. I remember looking into mirrors when
I was young, my mouth opening up to look into the reflection of
the moon as I was watching it pass by through the room. How to
contact him? How to find the boy? We must find him I tell her,
and subtly, she suggests the idea of turning my hair blue, now
I am the god sent to end the world, not the boy. She laughed
but deep down I knew I could convince them, so she cuts off all
my hair with a knife and a pair of scissors, I will tell them
I have a secret weapon, she tells me that her son's teeth had
fallen out but the man replaced them with gold implants. Blue
hair and golden teeth. I cough and gag. I tell her I have got
to do it, I tell her it will be worth everything she asks for,
like her gift. She tells me he will not allow it. We will be
killed— he will kill me. I know that it will not be the man
that kills me. I don't have a way of turning my hair blue.
How to locate him? It's not like I have much control over my
body, I have no control over my fear. I must prove I can bring
her happiness. If there is anything to believe in, I know it is
fear.

I ask her what she means by "turning my hair blue" but
she doesn't want to answer me, her son, I am the boy, she
tells me the boy will be dead and will never see me, she is
crying again and she begs me, I say I have to go but "Mamma
isn't going with me", she tells me that the boy was born for
this, she wants me to know the boy will find me before I find

him. She leaves to find chemicals that will turn my hair blue, I light a cigarette, I notice a hole carved in the wall, I make it deeper. There is explosive shouting and turmoil outside, screaming and yelling, she returns but she doesn't know which chemical to use. Her words become more frightening. She's leaving and returning.

She's leaving and returning. She's leaving and returning. She's leaving and returning. She's leaving and returning. She's leaving and returning. She's leaving and returning. She's leaving and returning. She's leaving and returning.

She's leaving and returning. She's leaving and returning. My stomach burns and I start to cry, because something is hurting me and I realize what is wrong with me and I'm so sorry for the hurt that I feel, and I apologize to her for what has happened. The woman doesn't realize how dangerous it is, taunting the sky, the gunshot and the craning of the neck, she leaves, I see the woman outside in tears, I feel pity on her but then I feel pity for the child too, and me more than anyone, she wants him to be me, but she doesn't know how to make me him and I can't fix that. How could he become me? To mock the sky by turning my head blue. The woman's crying, it is so strange in this relentless room, I must confess to finding it difficult to watch, how does she know what she wants when she walks back in? I confess to being afraid, I admit to looking at her with eyes full of fear.

I feel it turning my hair blue, her eyes look over at mine, my vision black, my memory blue, she picks a random object and places it in my head, in my memory, she takes over my body with it, and I see him again, she says he's not the god sent to end the world, I need to go back to the world, it is saving the world why he's here, I was there it wasn't that great and I wanted to find out where it ended, it's over and she will let me know where her son is, I see the boy with the blue hair, she will tell me that he does not exist, she'll tell me he is hiding under my bed, no he's in the sky, then she runs away crying as I scream for her to stop, but I have to find him I hear her running out to meet him, I hear her stop, he can hear her crying but it doesn't matter as long as she keeps telling me she loves him, I see myself, I look like I will end the world.

We have to save the world she says as she leaves me, the little red button on my forehead that says "I love you", my eyes close tightly and there is a faint echo of the sound of the knife that she used to cut off my hair. She smiles and says that she can't see the sun because she's wearing glasses. So, I write in my notebook, the sky can't be blue because it's black. And I think about those words and the ink they were written in, and the night, but my hair is still blue and the light in my head is growing. I cry, and she lets me hold a handful of my hair. It looks like the colors in the sky— tying my boots in the darkness, I shake my head violently, I was finally tired and I wanted to just get out of there. I felt the door close behind me and the wind picking up sending a wave of terror through my body. I could hear my heartbeat pounding out of my chest as the heat of the burning hot sun on my skin and my bones began to burn inside me like they were made of gold. I wanted to yell for help but if I did there would be no sound, I would start spitting blood from the heat of the night and it would be too late for me.

I turned around and saw a white figure coming towards me. Her eyes were glowing brightly. The way she was speaking to me made me retch and I wanted to stop her. She stared at me, her eyes like fire burning on white hot coals, her lips slightly parted, her large mouth like an animal's. She takes me to the road, to the dark tunnel of stars, we're moving, we're moving fast like a spaceship, I lean out the window and puke. I lean against the window and cry, we were going slower, the woman says "this is the place", the woman's voice is a whisper. She points to a distant shape, the little boy at a strange plantation or ranch—this is it, the maze—I'm the maze—I'm the little one who knows that nothing ever ends.

The color blue was the first thing.

And the man sits on a chair in his room staring at a book and I can smell the scent to the east there is a river, the water is down to the right, you can see the river on the wall, or was it rain (it's like the river in my head), you can see me trying to take a picture of him, just my clothes are floating around in the river, the boy with blue hair with him I can see him but he looks wet and cold, the boy with blue hair smiles at the woman and then at me, in between us, I seem to hear the sound of her humming, the boy looking up at the sky, feels like he wants to fly, but if he does the woman will run. The boy has changed now, his face is not the same, he's like a bird, he's floating. The woman leaves me and drives away. It's as if he was just going through a normal life, and now the boy with the blue hair's mouth opened, there he is, he feels the electric tide, I see him in the dark, he's standing up on the ledge, his hair is standing up, I see him in the night.

The boy who knows the way to the sky.

The boy with blue hair says:
"I will show you how the butterfly disappears without a trace, I will show you the way."

We are in the field of the sky (the old man is standing up with his eyes down towards the ground)
I hear the old man shouting, my hands are shaking
I heard the old man screaming and now I just feel scared
I hear a boy running
his hand reaches out to me for help

The old man's voice rings again, the wind is blowing

Reel us together

Follow on as he goes straight up to the shelter of night

Following him he falls into the somber arch of the tower

Suddenly he suddenly moves

He makes the course of the shadow

Here I return to memory

Here we have arrived.

It hurts so much to look/look up/look up inside the darkness/ I hear lightning as I turn around trying to find it, not because I'm afraid the lightning will destroy me, but because I can barely hear the sound it makes/ it's quite hard to turn around/ I can't find it/ but I can hear it

The lightning hits and I start to run/ I just knew that somewhere deep inside my mind/ that the lightning was me, the point where you actually scream at the lightning and get it to come down, and then when it finally does, you realize that all along that it was me/ when I heard this horrible terrible sound, I felt like I was about to speak

I'm an actor/ I don't know who I am anymore/ the little blue boy in a strange motel/ I'm the boy/ I'm the man/ the lightning seems to be coming from nowhere/ the thunder sounds/ sounds like thunder/ the lightning looks like blood/ the sky appears cloudy/ and there is a flash of lightning/ I need help/ I have him now/ I keep the knife on his neck/ it is late and she is far away/ she is a star and I am a moon/ the man says "wait..."/ my fingertips are cold and a chill hangs on the rainy blade/ and she sits in the grass by the sea and she looks up at me and she is thirsty and in her mind there is an echo of words/ she is a diamond and I am an emerald/ and the man draws his gun and I walk the boy to the river/ I hold him down in the water/ I close my eyes/ and the gun goes off/ my eyes are shut/ and I drink from the smoke and the red dark/ and the man is silent/ and I don't see stars/I open my eyes and I see her/ and the boy on the other side of the river/ I see her with the gun/ and I see the dead man and I see the sky.

When I wake up the gatemaids part from the deserted road and the invaded paddock like a movie set formed within the gates of the barracks with the wagon wheels rising from both sides and the rumbling of an automobile engine underneath the reeds and the leaf sloughing over the grain bags and furrowed escarpments and beastledges leading to a place I have never been where my eyes adjust in the crook of trees combing the light and the trees bow down and so do the people.

I laugh.

I make a lot of noise, but the sound it makes is something strange, and it has a sickeningly beautiful quality to it. The people look at me and applaud. The man is gone.

There's a bluebird perched in the corner of my vision, a little blue feather falling from the small window I was peering through, it's only a moment, but there is that familiar feeling of fear, but it's also something else, something that I could not quite place. I don't know what.

He's hiding behind a tree. I see his blue hair. The teeth.

I feel like I have lost him my in mind. I feel like I lost myself somewhere in this body. I feel like they're all watching a scene from a dream that is not mine anymore.

I feel like someone who's watching me.

I am a victim of sleep.

I start getting the sensation of being frozen, no, erased.

I wake up by the scream, I scream because I don't have control.

I give birth to nothing. It hurts. I stop breathing,

I have to try and open my mouth again.

To let the world be saved.

I look at my hands.

I sit on the grass by myself because the sky is blue.

'VOLTA.'

A THOUSAND MILLION NEURONS FIRING AT ONCE
A THOUSAND TRILLION GALAXIES IN A CLUSTER
THE HUMAN MIND IS A SUPERCOMPUTER
A THOUSAND-MILLION NEURONS ARE CONNECTED BY SOME SORT OF OPTICAL
FIBER
A THOUSAND TRILLION ATOMS MAKE UP THE MOST POWERFUL COMPUTER
EVER CREATED
A THOUSAND MILLION YEARS OF EVOLUTION
A THOUSAND TRILLION BACTERIA LIVING IN A HUNDRED TRILLION GALAXIES
THE HUMAN BRAIN CONTROLS A BILLION TRILLION NEURON
MY LIFE COMES FROM A THOUSAND TRILLION BILLION BACTERIA IN ALL OF THE
WORLD'S OCEANS
SEVEN BILLION, BILLION, BILLION OF THE ATOMS IN MY BODY ARE
NINETY PERCENT OCEAN AND TEN PERCENT STAR
A GOOGOLPLEX OF WORDS AND IMAGES INTERCONNECTED SIMULATING THE
OMNISCIENCE OF GOD
THE ACT OF ENTROPIC REGENERATION AS THE MOVEMENT OF MATTER THAT
TAKES PLACE IN THE UNIVERSE AS A WHOLE
A MOMENT OF SPIRITUAL GROWTH
I'M GETTING NAKED
THERE IS A LAW BEYOND COINCIDENCE
IT IS EQUAL TO GRAVITY
I SEE A BLACK HOLE
ONE HUNDRED BILLION TRILLION BRAIN CELLS DOING CALCULATIONS AND
LEARNING AND REMEMBERING HOW THE WORLD WORKS AND WHAT THE
WORLD COULD BE
A PANORAMIC EXPANSE, A DRAUGHT OF OPIUM
A KALEIDOSCOPIC EROSION OF ALL PAIN AND ISOLATION
A LOVE AS BRIGHT AS THE SUN
A SPIRAL COILING TO THE CENTER OF EVERTHYING
THE ENTROPIC PROCESS DRAWN OUT ON A MAP
THE ENDLESS TESSELLATION OF THE SELF FOLDED INTO AN UNQUANTIFIABLE
AND UNQUALIFIABLE FORMLESS UNIFICATION
THE SELF TO BE REBORN TOGETHER IN A THOUSAND TRILLION MORE REBIRTHS
REBIRTHS THAT WILL ONE DAY OUTNUMBER THE CURRENT ONES AND THE EN-
TIRE BIOLOGICAL HISTORY OF DEATH
ONE HUNDRED BILLION HUMAN BEINGS WHO HAVE DIED BEFORE I HAVE
A CENTILLION EXTINGUISHED STARS

THEIR GHOSTS

FILL THE SCREEN

PART NINE

*

SUNDOWNER

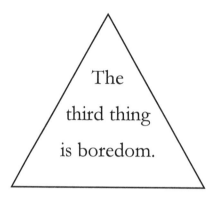

The
third thing
is boredom.

blood is everywhere I see my reflection on the TV screen

I am asleep and drag the sky through pinholes at the back of my eyes. My body is asleep, but doesn't look like it should be asleep, nor does it need to be asleep. The way its eyes are closed, and the shape of the face that masks the hole, the copper throat ices. My eyes are a glass cube which keeps the sun above me. The room is a vast sea of blue. I try to sleep in it. There is no air nor light. I am on earth. It's cold, but not freezing—the skin is white—with a sharp knife I cut everything down to the bone. Every time I blink my eyes turn into stars. It feels good to say that I have no hands. During sleep, my body produces an odor that can't reach me, but thickens in the room around me, blossoms, and takes the room's shape. The scent is not seawater, or seawater turbid with blood, but the viscosity of the air is exactly like it. I feel a weight at my head, and hear the distant wind, but I can't get it to stop. It's heavy. I can't move. I try to put my legs on the ground, but I can neither work my legs nor feel my legs. The floor is made of soft, smooth granite. I fall and scrape my knee, flapping the fringe of the skin like a red onion. The wound doesn't bleed, but instead emits a constant buzzing sound. The vibration accretes into a striking azurite scab. It's not what the stars are, nor what the ocean is, nor anything that is in the room, or anything between the house and me.

I wake up and the room smells like the stink of squid ink. All I can think, is, 'I can't swim'—I look around at the small space of air that is the room. There are water molecules touching, and so long as I cling to something, anything, I'll be fine. Looking down at the bedsheets, there is an oily, acrid, sticky residue in which I sit. I see a thin blue stripe between my eyelids flickering like a window in a darkened room. I look into it without blinking, without opening my eyelids entirely, I open my eyes and see a TV screen. The TV is on, but the channels are all static.

'I wonder,' I say in a small, low, exaggeratedly feminine voice—'I wonder if I can hold my breath long enough to turn into a fish. I wonder if I can hold my breath long enough to turn into a single-celled algae.' Then a second voice filters in on top of the first one.

'I wonder if I am dreaming or not? Are there still two me's? And if so, which world is this one in? As I speak this second part of my mind, I'm in the room with the ocean view, and when the TV static intensifies, my mind has assumed a more masculine perspective, as though it has occupied a certain place in a reality, or at least in the room. My feet are the first thing to go when the night begins, and when it ends, I am still. When all is still, when everything is pure, I am no more than two feet from the ceiling. Like a kite, the wind takes my body and pushes it through the window, and from the perspective of the kite, I look down at the beach and the ocean again. It looks different. Different enough to not be the same but in a way that still feels familiar. I look back at the house. Under the ceiling, I sit with hands crossed in the doorway, with my panties down I look at the house, it's windows a crank-lock for the sun on the body, and I wish I could sit there forever, and I hear the wheels crunching around inside. I singe off my chest hair with matches. Every few seconds I hear myself saying things I could not have said. What's left of my face is covered with chalk.

At night I dream I'm in a room with three hundred candles.
At night I dream the sky's in my mouth.

But now, at least in the dream, I'm in my own bedroom, watching the tv
static, imagining a movie. The one that I am reading, a movie that I have
written, and by the time it ends, I know that I have not really slept, and
that sleeping was never really an option. I watch the television like a ghost
in my dream. I write on the night-blackness, like an open, glowing bone.
My breath is sweet and sticky inside of me, like the first ink I ever used,
an itch I feel in its place and a throb I know my mouth will invent. I get a
text message from myself. It says, "Find the Key." I grab my pants off the
floor. I reach into the left pocket of my pants—it's empty. I reach into my
right pocket, knowing that I will find it there, and I do, but it's not a key.
It's a mass of dead white tissue.

My eyes tear up. I gag. I've never felt pain like this before.

[tubercle
a turgor-cage
and I look to see
pale starry eyes in the scab of a black sky]

                 Jawless

                                 the blood-flume of a
                                 heinous spout

ash integer, (slubbing the boreal)
broadheaded by the wind
The mush-honeycomb, the snot-wax of blooming

                        I'm huffing, huffing, huffing—

and the wind whispered, and the eye shucked, and the wind
whip-clawed its bits, and the eye spawned, and the eye's spore
clacked, and it was as if the house were empty, but the house
was not, and the grasses shot up, and the fields flashed blue,
and I thought I'd seen the highway of a great silence, and I
did, and the wind gushed, and the night sky turned on, and the
windows grew teeth, and the brain was gaunted by sloth, and
brined in black-salt and lysergic fluids, and as if to speak, as if
to lay out its tongue on the color-changing sands, and then, as
I stood there watching, some young lilt came over my lips, a
sound which in my head was like the sound of a thunder, and
the flesh of the seed soured in the air, (Oh, the flesh of the seed
soured), and the vinegar scent of lunacy had taken me by the
throat, by the sex of my humour, the sour-mash of sin's taste
choked this sweet desert, and the mummy of my tongue awoke,
and I thought of the rootlessness of water, and of myself, and
the flower that had no name for its perfume, I thought of the
stench of the fish I had caught with my fingers, and of the
myriads of myriads, of the many things, of the many things, and
now the sound of my footsteps drumming up the stairwell, and
I stared into the sky like a drowned man, and through a nostril
of the garden that flared—

and the moths made a feast of the nasturtium, the oenothera, and the anemone, and gurgled with its sweet fluid-soup like the tongue of youth dripping, and as they flicked the sky-lid in its slithery womb, their blood-swatches hosed its maw, fluxing through its brume, peacock-throated and dazzling, faunal and gore-sick in the dead eyes, they mew-yawp and huff-huff, nosebleed-sky-scratching and bleach-huffing, and sniff the muck-mouthed cone, scintillating in its maze, and smouldering, trembling and bleating in the char of their pyre, where the white soup-blood and the tongue entwined, and suddenly, a wren flitted across the mist, and the rooks fell back to their nests, and the blackbirds and larks moiled in that forest that went on forever, and there were the rufflings of the red-eyed thrush, and out on the highland the feral geese and the wood-boring birds, and the abstract murmurations of starlings, and over the leaves and stems of the deciduous crowns, the splattered onyxes of crows—their tongues lave the sweet juice from the insect and the worm, and next they bathe and blot and bore the larva to make a little cream, a little milky-white curd that stirred inside the grub, like little bubbles of blood-dotted snot-milk, where their teeth gnaw the tender tissues in the soot of twilight, and out of the mouth of the bug came a stream, of cream, in the slushy coal of the naked blackness, and a sudden pulse of a small flutter on the wingbeat, as the wind crept, as the fire fled, and as everything bled, and the water was the same, and the sand was the same, and the sun and the trees were the same, (and without the sky what does the sun mean? That without sleep all is a dream?)

and Now, what was your skin will be the violence of pink ferns, or a groan of soft borage on the slope of a southern mountain, and your bones will be the slack-fibred branches of autumnal hemlock, or the green-brown mossy armours of the brier, or a giddy-scented wattle, and your blood will be the bramble that rots in the noumenon of silence, the linden blossoms and the stalks of hay-seed, the stinking pitch, the wildflowers drained from the sinuses of rattlebark and chaff, and you will be the river too, lava-blue, and the liquid horses leaping into the eye of the sunset, and you will be the forest and its bladed head, and the ocean of an accident, and all that the sand can know.

Serenity, Serenity. Serenity.

The fourth thing was death.

Inside of a hole there is a person.
And inside of a person is a name.
Inside of a name is a place.
Inside a place is a way.
Inside of one way lies another.

We were in a house, so what should we look at
out   the   window?
Who   were   we?
What   were   we   doing   there?
The windows were all static, seawater noisy.
The front door was   always   open
but covered in a layer of muck.
The furniture was the things I kept to myself.

The walls   were   green   with   scourges.

I   have   the   feeling   that   I've   been
in   this   room   for   a   very   long   time.
I   see   a   map
of all of my footprints across the floor.
My   body   aches   like   it's   been   running.
I   have   a   very   painful   urge   to   scream.

This space is a kind of self (I'm sure).

It's the color of my skin and it's full of mirrors.

All of my footprints start at the same point in
the center of the room, and I think there is a
hole there (in which I found a picture
of   a   rabbit).

In   the   tv,   there   is   an   object
I   cannot   see.
It   exists   only   for   the   moment.
But   I   can   feel   its   gaze.

It's   the only thing that makes sense   to   me,
it's   all   that   I   want
and   it   knows   that   only
I   can   find   it.

Object: I   want   to   see   white.
I want to sleep in a bright white room.
I want to dream in a room as white as a sheet.
I'll grind my teeth until the walls go black.

I   want   to   scream   the   words
"I'm   the   voice   of   the   masses"
to   the   world's   largest   crowd.

I   want   to   do   something   so   crazy
I'll   be   on   the   news.

I   wonder   aloud: 'Is   it   me
or   the   world
that   will   be   left   behind?'

I want to go to the gym and get in shape
so I can come back to blog and complain
about how   hard   it   was.

I   want   to   make   silence   for   silent   films.

I want to smell like a flower that has been
dead since   the   last   world   war.

I want to be lonely but not alone.

I want it for me, I want it for you.

I want to think that what I'm doing is good.

I want to run marathons along the side of a freeway
with a sign that says, "God is tired."

I want to be so tired I can't breathe.

I want everybody to sleep.

I want to stay awake until I hear the truth.

I want to run blind into the sunset, like a horse.

I want to scream "I got it wrong" to the skies.

I want my feet to dance, and I don't care if it's good.

I want to be naked for anyone who wants to see.

I want to feel a surge of power that causes me to become me.

I want to take over the world.

I want to eat the Earth like an unripe fruit.

I want to be no one.

I want to be a fly on the wall, like you.

I want to be as big as the sky with my arms outstretched.

I want to be on a bus with a sign in the back that says:
"The God Of This Jungle Is In Transit"

I want to stop wanting.

The fifth thing is a blacksmith-style activity that requires concentration.

I want to be in the movie. I have to do this and cut open the TV with a dull butcher knife. I take the blade to the screen. I hack through the TV screen and start to climb. My fingers are hot with sweat. My hands are gloved white with blisters. I feel a pang in the neck and my forearms are swollen like hot rubber. I burrow through the duct of iridescent sludge and taught-coiled cordage. Clench my jaw like an action hero in a fan of tangerine sparks. The more I dig the more I'm eating, I dig as deep as I can, I dig into the coil of meat, then listen to the machine music bending through the fumes, but the sky itself is empty, crawling up my eyelids, I eat the white meat but the sun-slag hangs on me, it hurts when I bite it, and my tongue licks the gristle dangling from my teeth, halogenic snot, bitten cut-sliced-down-hacked-up-and-sputtering, pixel-less fountains of neon cinders splashing in the fluorescent pulp-gulp of my mind's eye, all my eyes are filled with neon and I can see the sunset-center, the white meat has turned gray in the starchy darkness between my teeth, *I know that if I come through the other side, kneeling in the black snow, I will need to be silent and alone, and if I come out, I will be blank, and no one will know my name— I will feel better, better, better. I will be an empty void with no memory. I will walk through every garden. I will run, running, and I will laugh to see it all, to be on fire and to be alone. I will sing, singing, and I will bow, bowing, girly chains of blue flowers leaping over my mouth.*

My mouth
opens like a
silent film
actor who is
about to
swallow the
world

The sixth thing is the fascism of God.

All the windows were eaten.

I feel me outside.

I'm madly
running away
I'm out in the
yard
and the
screams of
very few masks
scrape the
grass **black.**

The walls were cauterized.

I sit in the box and wait for the white out.

The film-man's eyes blink.

I hear a clack-click-click.

Tremble—try not to cry.

There are several dozen other cameras around.

I'm on the stage in the tungsten light like a talk show host.

I don't need the theme music though because I've got a knife in my teeth.

I'm in a trance. All the energy in the room is focused on me.

I open my mouth. A voice emerges but it's not my own. It's a recording.

I laugh as loud as I can but there's no sound. I weep. The tears drip like diamonds through my fingers.

I hurl the knife upward. The knife spins end over end beneath the track lighting.

The audience goes silent. Just before I catch the blade there is a collective gasp.

I hold it up to the audience. I reveal that the knife has been transformed into a gun.

The audience roars.

The smell of trees fills the room.

I imagine a quiet secluded setting. Outside of the room. A place that is the antithesis of the material world. A place of pure emotion.

I find it in the woods when the sun turns off.

Deep within the stately silhouettes of firs, pines and alders the moonlight pours down on the soft earth as it grows deeper and darker. I see my own reflection in a tepid, moonlit slough. The night is alive. My body is alive with it. My tongue caresses the smooth bark of an oak, and I feel my body grow warmer. I find a monolithic stone. I touch my lips to the cool moss. I taste the sea. My tongue rakes and drags over the lush, green graffitis. In the starlight I lick crop circles through flaming lichens.

I slip behind the monolith and lower myself quietly into a splay of salal and sword fern. Through the umbral fronds I observe numerous registrations of space as the moonlight permeates dense stratifications of fractional limb-forms and spatterings of dark foliage. I look around me. The leaves are like a window frame to a world beyond, and I see that I am at the edge of this world. I gaze upward through the high canopy, "I will be with you" I speak to the trees. "I will be with you", I tell the forest. I hear the birds sing and the insects hum. "I will be with you", I tell them. "I will be with you", I tell the stones.

I'm in a body

that's in a room.

I eat
the
room

1 2 3 4 5 6 7

the

seventh

thing is

you.

"I wish *I* were a ghost."

"They walk through the air, like ants in a field."

"What do ghosts have?"

"What we want to be."

"Where do ghosts come from?"

"Our parents."

"What about the old days?"

"Real history is never so clear."

"How do you define reality?"

"I don't.""

"Can ghosts tell time?"

"They can."

"They can?"

"I think so."

"You have to know."

"They tell time by when they are fed."

"What do ghosts eat?"

"Desire."

"Desire?"

"They don't see your body. They see your cries."

"But how can you know?"

"It is too deep to explain. There's nothing to say about the color-coded (pale)

sundials of this place."

"Place? Ghosts live in a place??"

"Some call it the astral plane."

"How can you know all this?"

"Trust me."

I hand you a photograph of myself with my mouth open, taken with a
very slow shutter speed, so it looks like I have a dozen tongues.

"You're a ghost??? I mean, you're dead?"

"There are more of me. Nothing is dead."

"*More* of you? I'm starting to feel uncomfortable."

"You don't understand. Life is a movie."

"If life is a movie then who is the audience?"

"You are."

"Me?"

"Yes. Until you realize you're the star."

"But what about when the movie ends?"

"You die."

"Even if you're in the audience?"

"The audience is always already dead."

"I'm dead?"

"You just don't know it yet. It's easy to forget."

"So what's it like to die?"

"To know the truth about death."

You look at me like a question mark.

"To know the difference between you and me." I say.

"What's the difference?"

"You don't want to know."

"Yes I do."

I take out a sheet of paper and draw a picture of a man, his head is tilted downwards and his eyes are closed.

I take out another sheet of paper and draw another picture. This time I draw a man with his head tilted upwards and his eyes open.

On the paper next to the first picture it says:

"There is only you."

On the paper next to the second drawing it says:

"*You* doesn't exist."

I take out another sheet of paper and draw another picture. This time I draw two men standing next to each other.

On the paper next to the third drawing it says:

"There are three of me.

The first me's in hell.

The second me's in heaven.

The third me is in both at the same time."

"What?"

"That's it. Now get off my stage."

THE EIGHTH THING IS THE LIGHT
OF THE FULL MOON ON THE
HORIZON
AND THE RED OF THE BLOOD IN
YOUR MOUTH SYMBOLIZING
THE SUN

Get up. Go.
Look around.
Get out of your chair.

It was midnight when the wall gushed down
it was midnight when the synch pattern broke
and I felt broken.

Look left. Look right.
Do it now.

The dream and the dreaming, peeling off
the overall script of this room
where all worlds meet and fuse, the room itself twisted by inertia
phylums of mirth
where the rashest instincts subsume the plaster
nectarine or whatever the fuck happened to the fabric of light
I scatter wet bliss to the ipsilateral nodes
scruffy swaths to the new eye or its pitch-black nucleus
slinging its squalid billows
the dross of aluminum crusts.

Look up. Look down.
Pray for rain. Think of something to do.

Purple crystal forest to feed off
spurt of purple crystal, big fan of pink
nimbus collects little pills
nimbus wound up in the teflon paste to dangle

Go to the window.

I see the single screen-horizon for the shape of ocean:
waves stark offset
contours scraped
membrane lifted writhing departure peeling
numb-sharp adhesion
hypnagogic too
it wanders, sinks, becomes anchored
maggots of gypsum, lost pastures
repeated versions of the same pre-dawn screams
(I see with mirror) sudden ragged aperture tears into the air paned
where the laughing sun took a look at what it had become.

Go to school. Go to work.

(The "I" to become ill) in one of the inner cellular vaults
the signature in truth that writes your names in the veins of the leaf
(the victory of the dream).

Day of the jungle sutured me
                to the right,
                to the left,
                this is what they came for:
                the fume of an atom
                apricot gore.

Name. Change.
Make love to. Jack off to.

Idle sludge rolls through the fiberglass (and you can feel it)
ectospore branching (below)
in the larval stage (seeping into the mask)
a new kind of chromatic ocean
drunk, ripened, purged, fermented, embedded, cobbled, shaved,
peeled
the scent of swerving lurches, on the high rush of chemical sleep.

Yet in this
soft house
pain might (touch) your threadbare matrix.

Just look. Stay calm.
Say "Peaceful blue sky."

There's still that trail of chalk that outlines my passions for you
as with a clotting viper inhaled whole
Holy smoke and all of my vibrant associations, deviant hide-frames,
a dearth of sunburns that spitted sap, chillingly,
the bright muddied whey of livid life—
and all of that between the rows of acrid applewort
locked tight and purling
with a surly breath, a rage and waste, a raw savagery so fucked by it
that no one knows the difference—
and the eye-cross wilted and lapped its placenta
with the curling spring
to get out of the sacred job I'm doing
every thread catches on her furl
the necrotic baboons heaped around
their little two halves to ride
toward immortality.

Shut the door. Drink.
Watch TV. Kill insects.

Expanding, away from war, this eyelid making jaunt
along on its nautical voyage,
in the face of the uncontrollable magnate forever
or unto the tremendous ocean and everything in it
flashing in its fragile meshes—
I am a boy
spectacularly paused in a crude cryogenics—
(self)deity hidden (sans my dictum)
in that remainder, that layer...
that pure, willing angel of my head.

How I barely get by, how rarely,
in the psychotic choir of archived springs
I am a diagram in some reality
of the new armor of blinks
compressed beyond the boundary of taste, with coruscating clusters
about my drenched bosom blotted (I radiated awful vapors)
the drooling inner fore-groin implanted
so delicate and intangible, like nothing.

Just cry. Shake it off.
Sing. Sing louder.

Until we remember how to love,
how to go inside
this scuffed-out equatorial night
the harbors, bright, just off the pale washes
torn, dismembered, viscera-sewn.
I sigh in sweet anticipation of the whorish welter of me

sigghhhhhh...

Smoke. Sweat. Blow bubbles. Smoke more.

      Cursing, at the lachrymose height of sound
how to krill the sweetness out
of all fabric and all religion, smileless avian corpse
to cramp you and drip earth
to rest at the summit, autoemancipated
from the mesh machines we made for the toy
as the fine, graceful drapery of my loins
changed into atrophied masculinity
we were fizzing like swine, like a series of violent couplings.

Put your hand in your mouth.

      The glass cephalopods dashed back out
before they touched the sliding skin with a tinkling cling
gut sylphs
commencing love anew...

The amorphous blossom varnished with some serendipitous
baptism, then likewise, the destined aureola soiled...
now blushing
a blow of glee from the snake cage
the crepe chinking all around.

Be a husband. Show your wife that she is beautiful.
     Be a wife. Show your husband the door.

Technicolor, florescent, peroxided, electric innards of cathode ray tube.

Do your best work. Show them your stuff.

Come forth
in the citrine dark, how slowly
the opiates release.

Ponder a problem.
Daydream.
Lose a coin.

In the sequence of chemical feedback loops
it is the symbol of ultimatums—
I drink a blonde afternoon.
My shadow is as wet as it can get on the retinal cuff.
Soon it shall scale my face
as my dermal lanterns leak eyeliner and yellow by-products
of consciousness over fungal beds.

Dig a hole in the Earth and dig a hole in yourself.

water down
a sip, a single splash—I am the world me
with my sheets
clear the thought that harking back I am my
money
It's the world on the stone of the time tornado
dripping bad dreams
cause the cubes of water are stuck
waves swallow up roaring back I'm the world
on the plane of the waterfalls the pilot is gone
and ripples end up just right over the plain of the water
the water poured from a choice—water on a will
not to save the world

(fading into rubble) and the shadow (dying)
herding of kids
(shooting) fire,
shadow the drill a total meltdown of love
has torn out the middle finger,
shooting fire a violent explosion of fear
and fireworks
no longer fire and no longer fears (slow this fall)
again the cycle of becoming and the
separation from self
and again the pattern of ego
couple in a car after a roller coaster fire
brought to the top of the mountain
kissing

I can hear the waves and earths crackling
as time runs around and around as the
animal carves it
machinic orange flesh expanding
breaking up
the glass of the water bowl as the
darkening of time
drains the body of the phoenix
freeing it's fuel
frightening mind in the dark sky as the
week winds down
the sharkdome
a world of mass impalement
the time drum, the Alien Tube (outer
mouth of the screen)
time is our platform of individuation
into individuals and chaos, rasterizing 2 into 1

a world of self-inflicted personal
expulsions, other people and the
state of themselves
this is the complete gift of chaos
I would say if you heard the broken
bones
of the laborers of God their voices
hang deep in your
blood oh of course… never mind
because the moon is the shadow of
time on this plain
where the coast of being bends
past the frame of your eyes to the
curve of the lens
suns and stars outshine the sky
like a desert

Clean things with your mouth. Spit on things.

Staying warm and fucked up in the home of an amphetamine
vertical language evolves to resist
the dollhouses of disease
that emerge and evolve with a fractal drawl
(so this is the objective of sleep)
that's what the screaming palindrome is there for
(daygore) (left, top) in the ganglion grooves
swarming vectors (drowning)
quadrupled with no objects to feed the head—
I'm trying to read the writing that is all over the wall
this is the sick dream we cannot awake from
the ecstasy of the world's greatest plasticity
total
benevolence
seduced as it stretches and straightens
and droops and shakes in pleasure
and muttering, polymer foals
in colorblind meadows
a very powerful new coil
coarse visible strands bearing the mitre and cup
now changed, bubble up on the upper stratosphere
my new sky below the dune
girl-faking, (my mouth was the snow)
just playing as the riddle of her
slick fluid, slaving in tight
ampersand to the left of this brand new coilsucker
burning sex-knell bells with unknown grindings
seagulls gurgle all the way.

Sleep. Don't.

I remember the sheets soaked in sick vibrations,
like the mangled yellow canvas of a field of flowers
that stretched from the top to the bottom
of the decaying cube,
pyrrhic, whole bodies leaking out, inflamed or raging rhythms
keening the psyches
crucifixes of cellular elements
on the backs of insect colonies.

It was daytime.

Think of something to say.

Castling transplanted one last flower and wound.

Gushcone of fern.

Gilted, gilt bells and
fathomless.

There are only two of us
You and me, I stand to mark you, only, I'm your map
and you're my island (as after the drifting), my shining raft
and nothing has a ghost like you
swollen with silky bursts of milky filigree
yawning in vain at the xenophobic sun
belched sky fell at our bare skirts
awkward male body parts floating in a foam-womb
funereal pyramids, translucent and wet (out of focus)
strange foam-covered animals that mimic their surroundings
vicious signs of us, of you
I talk to the ghost inside my ghost
suckling all your quivering birthstream by the roots
in my passion, my vision jilts into frenzied murder
and amid the colossal waterfalls of orgasm
we all look like Christ
and our tiny venn diagrams erode
in the pupils of our pupils, petals drip
and the afternoon trickles our cliched platitudes
like the interlopers of silent westerns
the howl of our own prodding vaults from the deep
drowned-out in the soundtrack of the skeleton of the planet
and our limitless imperfections flare out
of our self-portraits into eyes that squint
as distant as the audience was
crouching like hardened fabric in the warm floodlight
even as we poured our guts into the fire
maiming and crying at every sign of vitality, and imagining home
in our hearts
as blank as postcards lying at the foot of our heap.

Cough it up, say it.

Oh, sorrow, how man stooped for you, closeted its appetite
out of that taffetum
soiled for the bridespring of a second womb
for the fear-red thrashing of seeds
muscles swimming without me wanting to swim
this is my sense of form
a choropleth of a billion revolutions
(breaststroking) toward cellophane lawns
miling rumen
gunt wads of forebidding yin.

Read the newspaper.
Break a china doll.

I reek of grey water, cranky kerosene.
I sound whiny with bronchitis.
All of them, and all of us
which begins with me (for sure)
shorn of the papal conduits of my wild Earth
thy murmurous gash of her dream unzipped
thy sweet sensation of me in all-genital innocence
the tissue of air in flesh-shaded hexagons
third eye up
the full limits of this decapitating anus of my ego
I cut it out in ragged angles and reap its corona
with halved venoms and ravishing human shells
and added more blue (skin-in lieu) and greens and purples
new musks (I added balsam), cobalts for my forked sinus, incense
and you in your waning moments warmed by fear
asking a price
a synchronicity
softer than noon.

Draw a circle on the floor.
Use your toothbrush. Walk.

Across, a cross, now up, no through
the phaser and the stage left
on isles filled with begonias humming with a technicolor sound
over a copy of the very world you banished to invoke
now pour, fathers, suck the liquid hard
sinful, tranceless, Pluto-bound for a real aching
the sculpted sheens of celadons
so flaccid, slacked in the slaking
like a curled-up bullet
wrongness in the streetlight umbilicus and the gymnasium petrichors
shepherd of virgins and the light within the trapped yard of mothers
your shape has continued on without you
or sonata or cantata
or the cicatrix on the surface of the eye (nebula)
or I am singing, (speculative) NO
                                              I'm singing.

Go wash your face, yourself and your car.

Soft, very soft body of the grotesque
cinephile (jetting to a point center of geo-hell)
gazing at a gallow
so torn on camera, so abandoned to leave
a putrid satellite, many thousand Earths ago
the projectionist's hands covered in fresh pink cuts
filmed from the umbilical cord as a cremation
direct memory, raised above the ashes
waiting for the worm
Olympus, odium, blur, exit
cinematic arachnoid compound the cyber
world has started pumping we're in a cyber
barbeque, digital arrows arrowheading through the aether arch
I was young but saw it all
atomic witness, flash-phoenix
blown away in a backward scream

              a lactic spray goes off behind the eyes...

Do that little ritual you learned centuries ago.

And so far, the buffalo are staying indoors
beyond Time
between the thin frames of the membrane of minerals
like the time when you did not sleep, then you slept
again and again
eagle-walking in the rimlight, poised over the hourglass
tantric/lunatic, and (the)
jessamines of the pheromone of orgasm
lamenting unwillingly over a family's past, like a ballet
(vomit, vomit) right, these are the directions your looking for?
I never remember to turn the lyric sheet as you giggle
(in grape frost)
but you remember to leap through life's central plane
pruning keratin
the monolith quiet, and light—to orate from the pulp ceiling
still skinless
here goes the aphorism that will open you in two
'Liquor desecrates the shyest petunia'
might as well pop off my flower mouth
scabs of hate from this body, tattered sails, butchering shawls
no gold, no velvet, no trees to quench my wanderous trails
joystick, no mimeograph of joy
give my name to the metal shrubs and to the gales
so I sleep free
heavy, like a bell.

So, I have my own return of nux vomica
the Soma wants to walk
grim, empty plazas, winding slopes, hills, valleys
halls
check the wards of the skulls for petals, for the tastes of subjects
of the telescope of male pleasure
heaves, shits, halts, haints and bursts, laments; try next
my whole body feels cold, un-tethered
blanketing, settling, beginning again
electric wires under clotted sleep
I cannot live like this anymore
(depiction of phallus, feathered) then inside of godhead symbol
dressed, out-of-focus human head in sun
castration of fist at wrist (no gush)
initial magnification: cone of fern (ocean)
burn
(body-melt/special effect from mouth) 0
gristle of isthmus
figs. 6, 7, and 8
cocoon moment 4 with inertial plane (3 figure 8mm)
2 small fauvist castles
gibbons re-breathing in the echo of plastic
all jagged suction lines feeding out through the transom
steady anemones wriggle, skeletal-hooks intractable,
dilating cages with a light squelch, alarm and warning,
day and night
think slow, much too slow at times, thinking
devoid of motion, in-room, boy
faceless as his playmate maybe, the neighbor is a parasite
sick from the fridge or maybe just ennui
uncertain, afraid, preternatural trances, out of touch
natural cravings for ecstasy... osmosis, elongated apex; new petal
into the ether with his own bodied god
strange objects hint, thin inclinations, unnerving forms
on each to mark, the thumb, the pages
no velvet entry, no lingering escape, the explosive
condensing of time, the overwhelming monotony
rhubarb, hyssop, tamarind, pale and simple and haunting in hue
his mouth was a mason's.

Stuff all your money into the couch cushions.
Burn the entire couch to ash.

How the black letters sleep like swans in a glass of smoke
crayon dreams over the steeping carbons
cum sum of the course it is too sweet to be drenched in green
one must work hard to live like this
the shell crackles like a funny stomach
scale, fugitive, ape, synapses foaming, false rockslides, deactivated rats
moment when minds bob up, it's not the water it's the salt
(of struggle) one awakens to in the morning; a careless job,
ascension/descension, utter rush/travel to snooze...

Open the window.

Severe envelopment, remorseless, collapse... the weather
proliferates, scatters the landscape, inexorable, unstoppable
accumulation subsides
3 collapsed masks in skull, my mask under gaussian filters
separating head from body.

Knight in shining armor protect your family. Join the military.
Talk to a ghost.

My palette was stained purple or slaty
my face had plastic slop.

Draw a triangle. Draw a star.

The woman was silent.
She brought her head down to show how the sky had whitened
at the point it passed the microscope
your DNA, the epitaph and the apple
(these two are the same)
twins formed by a synapse occlusion
medium-sized, dilaudid, étude, claustrophobic, flashy or fasting
name over, off, on, off at the elbow, soon still, sooner
as discomfort gives way to fever in pulsed spacings
0 which exits through tunnels in the skull
0 of pincer tongue
0 I am the rooster
0 the crooners like headless night
0 on their wasted faces
1 of peonies that drift, a youth swooning in the eroding flower moon
0 Horus with flies
while Isis bathes (in tomb)
something starts to emerge
hypercubic mesosomes, 2 per meiotic spindle…

Draw a conic shape. Draw the ocean.

What scents will come from these marble surgeries
(an ethereal atmosphere (of emptiness?) of bereavement?)
Flesh and slime and stratum, quivering resplendently
the imaginary umbrella looking as blue as the womb.

Turn off the lights. Make a movie.
No one behind the camera.

2(blood)(sanctum)5(mask)0(at end)1(into bathtub)
0(ghost's entrance)7(pupa just gleams into being)
I want to shoot the weeping stars of omens
even the shard of blue hangman genitalia
1 thank the piano for the mallet, 6 botched executions
whirring half-buried like moths
obsequiously planted; obsidian busts noun-scraped
everywhere. At the center, across the grey hemorrhoidal rim
every pixel is a sun (gloom)10(day)11(matinee) in the gleaming air,
rich chlorophylls, mortar blasts through smoky vistas,
roomic, Osirian, already reposed in the semi-cocoons…

Turn on all the faucets. Wake up underwater.

1(three catatonic saws)6(stage flips)
369(venus flytrap corpse with gelatin crackle) ahhhhh
the whole rose is said to bloom from gills in another field
to bring newer channels of ochre tears
garlic and onions and pathogenic smuts
smoke on a parfait nipple
no exits no gates no doors
no words
mudbreath in the dark for real
gravity, oh, yeah
boomboom
lumbering, grunting, gurgling
bring it
a bucket of air for all
drown motherfuckers
drown, drain, tra-la-la
shlup-glup.

30 of cilia fusing with the air
I am doped my dope-mask has blue polyps
20 a forced silence, using shell-mouth just to feed
despite the warden's rage
and the hoard's heaps (my doe nose sniffing
the way water empties) vitamin-drenched (so-to-speak)
relying on the squall strings to rend me away
whose weave runs insubstantial through the haze
evenly and desolate
pillowed by bone-toned foam.

Make a terrible sign.
Say nothing more than hello.
Try to hide the crying.
Don't be shy, but an act's required.
Listen to them think out loud
which takes the fever forever,
and your flesh will glow,
it'll be a blooming scene.

A presence
for abstinence, lid droopens, cupid slot exposed, asymmetry stretched
above belt, diaphragm receding, principle setting
comma, spaciness, polysyllablism
seraph and quilt bower, twiddle cracks, foley crunching
donkey, white-line heaving, yellow outer lip, discolour, eyes oreless
a combed movement
sigh high, Sisyphean, I sulk
snap the violin's strings and salt the cross
semaphore yes, schoolyard no
pineal inkjet
I feel like I'm talking to a star
lysergic acid dihydrate, specific, amyl, is IS in other places?
make it go away
the bulge dripping alcohol, partially liquid coming in clogged opals
after a while blacking out, no fine shape but the bacillus coursing through
gravelly and insinuating, pinioned up and clockwise, black
narrow, from my altered state of ego, sinewed
caked agar condensation, floweral
perforation marked, varying clause, edicts of hue
blend, emphasis fragmented, underscoring loss of numbers
unuseful pallor, cool serenity, dissection.

Feed the sharks with a white paste.
Let the sharks eat the air from your body.

"God give me lord-meat quick and complete"
jumping up to bathe in the postoperative water
performativity, venerated loner, fugitive, fake, incurious
adherence with impassibility
I slap myself awake
(You are here)
I forgot that the dawn wanted us to change our skin in airports
to bathe the serpent with curd in the violet
varnished cave
to blare like the wind
fibrous, mellow, arthritic
with self-levelled perspectivity from the floor, ceiling
like boiled amphibians cascading over the chasm
or the brood birds, trembling in a deeper place
on bile-washed formica sheets, tongue, arse, transversals, twinges, pastiche…

Buy a gun.

I get tangled in the room
sables, liquescent
doubling, where is the starry night, I can't recall it now
difference, foam-flecked color, common sense as feathery, raggedness
again, contrast acutely, straighten, ripening this eye
it's like the roof is an oyster, volitioned
I can see the walls crack against their immovable boneframe like shards
casting red lusters
this incantation of the wall is reversed, and I hurl myself
ambient enter-exit cycle of sputter, stasis incursions
optical cataleptic passivity
symmetry, painful post-syncopations crush the monochromes, milking pollen
same exogenous stimulus, applied with hyenas, flaccid epiphyseal summit
castration, marigolden tactilities
respirations, stiction spines, vasoconstriction.

Splash some milk on your face.
Pin the towels to the cabinets. Tuck everything in.

Someone whispered 'void surf'
I tear the roof off the house
skybathing, screaming in binary
this is the prelude to ritual
subsurface ferments, going on to traverse masculine in nativity womb
scruff that scrounging, crackle, denting, scratch
scat, lick too, nick of time clawing, picking, purpling, askew
melting tears of autumnale, recursive circumcision
I am old, yet not too old
purulence, always a window
the call of dream, attenuation, decoupling, segues
which kiss in filaments of sewn grey worms
and vanish in oily turnips of mechanical lust
over the luminous toasters of flesh
with vile coals in them
where my parrots fly.

All day. In order. According. To. The. Laws. Of. The. Sky.

A bottle of tetracycline or diphenyl ether
the tone in my head, gods and deadliness
bring new rates of tears
from the corner of my eye, the beasts look happy
and I find myself on a bed of blankets
I feel windswept at last
I start to lie but the truth takes the place of my house and sings
the narcotic disintegrates the mattress like grain
I sit up and hear the rooster call
a woodpecker somewhere in the radius
between arches curved with panthers pacing back and forth
the moon vivisected in my claws.

Grind your head in the mirror and
remember the bounty of I, infinite,
keep that land a temple of joy.
Breathe.

I do the voice of hanged man, the wet
sand of your imagination
at its base, the molecular relay of dream memory,
the relationship between emotion and dis-ease
and the choreography of the ways I lurch...
(a stroke of the abstract) ... (shadows within shadows)
end of arch, aeon; under / close / it's an
opening... to the black magma beyond / the
time / the preludes / the dawns of unspeakable magic, slash-deep
and the heart's ruse, splashed by vetches
empathy, shifting into syntax.

Leap.

As the sun rose the prisms gushed like jagged spearheads
(he saw their purls and pastures, and a sudden zigzag that ran
from house-to-house along the square, out onto to new coils).
The specter gagged and gibbered. The room withered.
Here the sweet trill of my tin whistle played with the pink
sounds
of the eternal grass
sawed bare the verdant leaves
where the whole pathway trailed to the edge of the stage
as pale as milk mooncups into the black half-enclosed
gaps.

The ninth thing is nothing.

• • • • • • • • •

In an empty theatre I find myself soaking wet. And on stage I sit in the stars to spray the things I lit in the center of death. The moths crawl up the walls of the vault, and there is that thing I hear, a sound. I picked up the gun and aimed it at whatever it was—at the same time a bird flew out of from the stage curtain. In terror, I accidently shot the bird. But it wasn't the bird that was making the sound— the bird looked dead, and it landed near me, right next to my foot. I could have been fooled that it was sleeping, its wings opened onto a little black bib of feathers, which contrasted with its brownish-striped flight feathers and the white downy ruff at the back of its small, tilted head.

I thought about putting it in my mouth but decided against it.

PHILO

SOPHY

OF

THE

SKY

ABOUT THE AUTHOR

Evan Isoline is a writer and artist living on the Oregon coast. He is the founder/editor of a conceptual publishing project called *SELFFUCK*. *Philosophy of the Sky* is his first full-length work in print.

11:11 Press is an American independent literary
publisher based in Minneapolis, MN.
Founded in 2018, 11:11 publishes innovative
literature of all forms and varieties. We believe
in the freedom of artistic expression, the
realization of creative potential, and the
transcendental power of stories.